C000294932

ACKNOWLEL

I wish to express my sincere gratitude to Mr Reece Beckford who has worked tirelessly through his college studies and exams to give me the most beautiful music to accompany this book.

You have been a rock in which I have leant on so many times, it has been a hard 2 years for us both and I cannot thank you enough for your time, effort.

I would like to gratefully acknowledge Phil, who has been a variant of amazing and patient and an absolute star in my life picking up my pieces and still been able to smile back at me. You gave me the time and space to write my dream and give me chance to do it all with no fuss.

I would like to thank my friends Calvin James and Hannah Halford, who without them I would have no ending to my book, there quick creative minds put together gave me a tear jerking fascinating ending and I cannot thank you enough for your time, energy and brains for your creative thoughts.

Last but far from least, I owe an enormous debt of gratitude to my Co-Author Marc Boyle- who joined my team last minute, and has been a constant source of joy to work with I thank you for your strength to endure me, when the days of procrastination was in full force you turned me back to the book.

This book was made from the heart of myself and my daughter faith, who without her, would have lost the will to live, but seeing her every day gave me renewed hope to carry on and get this book finished.

"Feel"

She stood there staring into her champagne glass asking herself why she ever came. Looking around the magnificent building Rose could not help but feel exposed due to the vast space around her and the strangers littered around the room. Beautifully structured marble carved ceilings loomed above her and her vision was obscured by intricacy in paintings that dated back centuries. She was surrounded by such elegance from the building and the array of colourful dresses that lightly dragged across the hard granite flooring. The building structure was of pearl with flecks of white pristine marbled walls which as she ran her hand across she could feel every sensation of a bump and scratch that had been left there over the decades from soldiers and messy love affairs. She imagined the drama that would unfold over the centuries, the walls that would have felt passion, anger, and lust.

The building was so tall that the voices of everyone echoed and bounced off the walls and concrete columns yet, it was hard to hear what anyone was saying. Watching lovers kiss and others hold hands only exacerbated the uncertainty she felt about everything in life. Taking one last sip of her champagne, she began making her way through the crowd.

As she walked through the large arched entrance, she froze. She could feel her heart pounding against her chest and a sudden sweltering heat came over her. There he stood in a blue velvet jacket with his gold-rimmed glasses and his left hand gripping a whisky on the rocks. Running his hands through his hair, that always flicked back into his tanned face, his blue eyes scoured the unfamiliar crowd. Rose threw herself against the wall her heart now in her throat. As she squeezed her eyes shut hoping he didn't see her, she could feel her head spinning out of control, whispering to herself,

"Not now please not now." She forced open her eyes to see if anyone was staring at her erratic behaviour, but luckily no one was. She knew she needed to get away- fast. Taking one step forward felt like wading through mud and she fell to her knees.

"No no no, not now" Rose muttered gradually getting annoyed with herself.

Gripping a glass table to steady herself, she pulled it down causing it to shatter across the floor. The noise of the glass shattering overwhelmed all of her senses until everything went black.

A SIGHT TO BEHOLD

Upon awakening she found herself lying on the floor, her head supported by a jacket. As she lay there attempting to get her bearings a face slowly emerged over hers- Rose covered her face.

"No no no no" she whispered to herself.

"Well as I live and breathe- Rose?"

"Yes" she whispered into her clammy hands, still covering her face.

Sebastian gently pulled her hands away.

"There you are. It's okay sit up drink some water."

Rose slowly began to sit up against the settee; her head pounding and her thoughts racing, they were in a room alone...

"Here take a sip you need to drink water..."

He sat down by her side.

"So you're here...finally..." Sebastian murmured with a fleeting smile on his face.

She turned to him with her head down,

"Look Sebastian, you don't have to do this..." Roses nerves betrayed her as she stared into her splintered and scratched palms.

"You're right let's not do this here...there is a lot to be said but not now, not here. Come home with me it's forty five minutes away?"

Before she had time to reply Sebastian put his finger under her chin to raise her head, forcing their eyes to meet. Rose could feel her soul melt and her stomach flipped, his crystal blue eyes and his soft finger under her chin felt like home to her...but the voices in her mind screamed otherwise.

He kissed her delicately on the lips; Rose closed her eyes and breathed in his familiar scent.

"I'm sorry I just..." Rose stuttered

Rose tried to get up and fell back down; she had cut her arm and hands where the glass had shattered on her.

"Let me help you up," grasping her back gently, Sebastian eased her to her feet.

No words were spoken. He helped her up and as he did so she rested her head on his shoulders. He kissed her neck and whispered something in her ear. Upon seeing her puzzled look he simply smiled.

"In time my love in time"

Rose just nodded, she felt too weak to question anything. He walked her to his car opened the doors for her after helping her down the stairs. Sebastian's driver stood by the car and as he looked over and his face brightened with a smile.

"Nice to see you again Rose"

"Thank you Ralf it has been an awfully long time hasn't it"

"It has indeed"

He opened the car door and Sebastian placed Rose gently into the back seat. Ralf took position to drive and Sebastian sat in close to Rose where she rested her head on his shoulder.

The bustling sound of the city seeped into rose's thoughts; she could not believe she had met Sebastian again after all this time. When they had finally arrived at Sebastian's apartment, he opened the door taking her hand. He told Ralf to go home and rest, he had a busy day tomorrow. The rain had stopped but it was still cold so Sebastian took his coat and wrapped her in it; he led her up the stairs to his door and guided her in.

Sebastian nodded to the security guard whilst Rose bowed her head.

"What's with the bowing head?"

"It's a habit I have if I'm shy" she smiled.

"Arghh right so you're shy" he said playfully.

"Yes if you haven't noticed," she said with a smirk

The lift came and they both stepped in, he was on the top floor pent house suite. Rose raised her eyebrows imagining the view he must have of the city of London.

"How long are you in London for?" Sebastian turned to face Rose.

"However long you want me for." Taking her chin in his hand he leaned in gently kissing her on the lips. She stayed still cemented in pure delight and breathed deeply as every sensation in her body came alive. His touch was delicate and his kiss was divine, she had waited a long time for that feeling again. But she wanted more, her body was aching as he went in for another kiss and she couldn't help herself. She kissed back harder, gently biting his lip and in doing so Sebastian moaned lightly in enjoyment. His body shifted closer, and she leaned into him, kissing became heavier her breathing was deep. He moved his hand across her arm but just as he was about to slip her shoulder strap off, the lift jolted to his apartment.

Rose stepped back and wiped her mouth, whilst Sebastian straightened his tie and jacket. The doors opened and a couple was stood there, Sebastian nodded to both of them, he grabbed roses hand and walked her out of the lift. She smiled, bowed her head as she walked past the couple, her face beamed red. She took deep breaths and walked close to Sebastian, finally at his door He turned to her smiling, slowly opening his door they both fell in laughing. She hid her face shaking her head.

"Could you imagine if we didn't hear the lift stop, that couple would have had a shock?"

"I know lucky for us" she giggled.

"Okay, Let me show you around" he walked off and Rose followed she looked in awe of his pent suit it was stunning.

A light and delicate décor surrounded her. The white and cream sofas looked like you could melt into them. A grand fireplace that was already alight, curtains closed. His bathroom was marbled and a shower that could fit in ten people. The guest room was massive with silk bedding and cream carpets.

He took her hand gently and guided her into a closet where there was a change of clothes. They were Sebastian's but Rose did not mind a bit.

"They're are my clothes if you don't mind wearing them I don't have any ladies things here it's my palace of solitude from when I finish lectures and talk shows and get some down time. My hideaway shall we say."

"Fair enough everyone needs quiet time," she said whilst stripping off her dress.

"You can grab a shower fresh towels there or just get changed if you like are you hungry?" Bearing in mind, it was nearly midnight and all she had eaten was an olive from the party. She was ready to eat.

"Yes please I'm starved"

Sebastian handed a menu over and said.

"Take your pick; I'll look at the menu after you I'm just jumping in the shower make yourself at home the TV is over there." Waving his hands towards the beautiful set of drawers where the TV was above

"If you want to watch anything I'll be back in a mi," Sebastien said as she looked over the menu salivating at the delicious array of food.

Tearing her eyes away from the menu Rose watched as Sebastian went to the bathroom hoping to catch a glimpse of his body but no such luck. She walked into the guest room and opened the closet to see Sebastian clothes hanging there. His musky cologne lingered. She grabbed his shirts and breathed in deep with a smile.

Flicking through his clothes, she picked out jogging bottoms and a jersey top.

Dropping her dress onto the bed she walked into the living room that looked like something out of country living magazine. She opened the curtains to find a balcony overlooking London and gasped. With twinkling lights looking back at her she opened the door that luckily wasn't locked, surprised she flung the doors opened and stepped out on the balcony welcoming the cool air on her face as she looked over London. The night sky was a blanket that quietened the bustling city below and captivated Rose's attention. She felt a hand snake around her waist and she jumped.

"It's only me," he whispered as he leant into her neck

My God he smells amazing, she thought to herself.

"Aren't you cold?"

"You're keeping me warm" she smiled

He hugged her closer to him and all Rose wanted to do was hold him. She turned to face him and he looked deep into her eyes.

"Do you know what you're eating?"

"Yes I do I've written it down by the phone"

"I'll have my usual I'll ring it through now".

Sebastian padded back into his apartment, pulling his towel tighter around himself. As he was on the phone, he made silly faces whilst ordering which made Rose giggle.

"Any drinks?"

"Yes red Wine please"

Rose turned back to the view of London peering down to see people waiting for taxis and couples talking, hugging in the cold, sheltering each other. She had a warm feeling inside her. Sebastian hugged her from behind again running his hands down her arms. She sighed with happiness as a familiar feeling of calm came over her. He delicately kissed the nape of her neck, putting her head to one side he kissed her ears lightly. Rose moaned he ran his fingers down her arms slowly making the hairs stand on end she shivered.

"Are you cold?"

"No" she whispered trying to control her breathing.

He kissed her neck again running his tongue along her shoulders gently smoothing his fingers up her arms, they intertwined fingers.

She turned to face him, he kissed her heavily on the lips and she ran her fingers through his hair, her body aching her lips and tongue grasping for more, she was about to take his towel away when a knock at the door caught them both by surprise

Rose looked over his shoulder, Sebastian stopped they both laughed and looked at each other.

"Second time tonight," he said with a sigh.

"I need to compose myself," she said feeling her body pound with desire. Sebastian tipped the waiter and brought the food over

"What did you get?" Rose asked peering hungrily over the plates.

"Just something light, bacon sandwich and crisps"

"Ahh yes I remember you like your bacon sandwiches," she smiled. They both took a seat at the kitchen table comfortable in silence eating their food.

Rose broke the silence.

"So what have you been doing for the past one and a half years?"

"Lecturing, book signings, T.V…" he stopped talking, silence fell once more and he turned his body to Rose. "I've been thinking about you, its sounds cliché but since that night..." his voice trailed off. Rose took his sandwich out of his hand and placed it down on his plate.

"I honestly thought you were crazy when you said if it was meant to be we need to meet under better circumstances."

"Are you in a good place?" he asked smiling.

"Yes I am"

 He looked unsure.

"I am" Rose nodded reassuringly at him.

They smiled at each other before he got up and walked over to the guest room to get changed, but not before shouting ..."you look amazing in my clothes "she smiled and lowered her gaze.

"Thank you they're very comfortable, and you're a gracious host Mr. Lawrence." Sebastian came back out in slacks and a plain white top and sat back down by Rose

She stopped eating and looked up to Sebastian with a question lingering on her lips, she finally spoke.

"What is this Sebastian? The feelings, the emotions it's just all new to me." Sebastian sat pausing for thought.

"I truly don't know Rose but it feels right. Why don't we just take our time and see what happens the feelings are there we can't deny it."

"It's comfortable, it's like I'm home," she said smiling.

They both moved to eat their food on the sofa and he turned the T.V on. Rose rested her head on his shoulder her eyes weary and her body ready to sleep. After a while Sebastian felt her head go heavier he looked down to see rose fast asleep.

"Rose?"

He looked at her peacefully sleeping, he smiled at her lifted her head and rested it against the settee back he put his glasses down and picked her up and carried her to his room.

Day broke through the curtains, the sun shining warmly and the room filled with heat, Rose woke and had to shield her tired eyes from the peeking sun.

Looking across from her, she saw Sebastian still asleep. She leaned over and gently kissed his lips, he stirred and turned to Rose

"Morning to you too" she said with a cheeky smile.

"Good morning" rubbing the sleep from his eyes

"You passed out on me last night"

"It had been a long day," she laughed

"You and me both, I'm just going to grab a quick shower." He took the covers off himself with hesitation and walked over to the bathroom slowly.

She sat up, and watched him walk over to the bathroom door; he looked over his shoulder to give a smouldering smirk to Rose, she giggled and as he walked off he stripped off his shirt and threw it over his head. He turned the shower on and she caught his shirt, she put it to her face, and breathed in deep. She carefully removed the clothes she had slept in and walked over to the shower shutting the door behind her. The water felt amazing on her skin. She grabbed the gel out of Sebastian's hands and lavished her body with bubbles- the smell was a delicious fruity concoction. As she was rinsing herself Sebastian just looked on smiling from ear to ear.

"You don't mind?"

Sebastian replied "Share my shower of course not…" with a playfully sarcastic tone.

Sebastian gently grabbed her shoulder and turned her as he kissed her back. She could hear classical piano music playing in the background. It was his alarm going off from his phone. He grabbed the shower gel, poured a generous amount into his hands, and began washing her back, slowly massaging her buttocks and making his way round to her stomach and thighs. Rose moaned in glee and turned to face Sebastian to see his body; his stomach muscles gleamed in the shower and she ran her fingers through his wet hair.

She grabbed the shower gel and began soaping his front slowly moving her hands around his pecks and abdomen enjoying the feeling of him. Sebastian moaned and lowered his head as she kissed his chest, but as she got lower, the doorbell rang and his phone started ringing.

Sebastian turned around, "What NOW?"

"You best get it." She giggled

As she stood there, her body desired aches for more and her fingers desperately wanted to linger on his skin. He kissed her and got out of the shower, quickly grabbing the robe that was hanging on the door. Rose carried on showering without him, washing her face in the warm water she thought how amazing she felt, how sexual she had been over the last few days and how confident he made her feel. It was a joyful feeling and this sat well.

Sebastian answered the door, it was the bellhop Tony, giving him a telegraph letting him know of his schedule for his tours also informing him of his flight at 2 p.m. Meanwhile Rose stepped out of the shower

"Are you okay?" she looked on as he packed his bags

"Yeah, I have lectures in LA tonight."

She carried on walking to the guest room to get her dress. Sebastian walked in behind her

"You're more than welcome to stay here Rose"

Smiling with glee she said, "thank you I'll pick some bits and pieces up from my place and bring them back over."

He walked over and unchained his keys passing them over to Rose. Silence fell between them, she looked at him not in amazement or a wonder of why, but a look of understanding. It was a binding contract of trust. Rose threw the keys in the air and caught them, smiling she carried on getting ready whilst Sebastian walked away to carry on packing.

"Do you want any breakfast before you leave?"

"Yes please" she shouted back from the bedroom as Sebastian handed a menu to her. She knew already what she wanted so she put on her gown and began drying her hair.

"Do you need any help?" Rose shouted out of the bedroom.

"No I have everything in order."

Sebastian was writing a note for his housekeepers when the doorbell rang to announce a breakfast tray Rose couldn't help but think that if she got into a hot moment with Sebastian again they would have been stopped, she giggled at the thought as they hadn't been given a break. Sebastian pulled over the breakfast and both of them tucked in. No words spoken nothing forced as they looked at each other smiling, eating away in silence. Rose felt something click, it felt right to her silence spoke a thousand words and this one word was comfortable.

They both finished up, Rose tidied away the plates, walked over to Sebastian and kissed him on his head.

"Are you going?" he said concerned.

"Yes I have a house to attend to and to come back here I'll catch a taxi."

"No no use my chauffeur?"

"Umm okay" she said with uncertainty

"Brilliant" he said with a glowing smile.

Sebastian stood up leaned over the sofa and came face to face with Rose. He stared at her and gently kissed her lips, she closed her eyes and sighed at his tender touch, her body ached for more.

"I'll be back in two days you're welcome to stay here and the chauffeur is at your disposal so do as you will. Put anything on my account you'll find the information in my office and any problems give me a call. He handed Rose his mobile

"Only in emergency okay?" He asked with a stern look.

"Yes" Rose replied nodding quickly.

She turned away and out of the door, as she closed the door on Sebastian she felt something missing but she carried on walking down to the car. Ralf stood outside and opened the car door for her tipping his cap to her

"Good evening Miss Banks where can I take you?"

She smiled to Ralf, "Fifty nine Crescent Way"

The chauffeur nodded and asked, "If I get lost can you guide me?"

"Of course no problem"

"Thank you, Miss Banks"

Ralf never lost his way and he pulled up to her drive in almost no time at all.

"You did well"

"Thank you I remembered some roads from last time it came back to me"

"Well thank you Ralf you're a gentleman"

"I'm taught well by a true gentleman"

Rose smiled "he is that"

Ralf ran around the car and opened the car door for Rose who got out and hugged him.

"Sebastian said that I can drop by any time at his house, I will be packing to stay over tonight so is it okay if I call you for a ride later?"

"Of course yes by all means," Ralf said as he got his pad out and scribbled his number down.

Waving to Ralf she looked up at her dilapidated house and walked to her door. Something didn't sit well with her she felt something was missing Rose felt her pockets and her chest she had her, phone her keys her money but this was a different feeling. She continued opening her door, walked in and ran upstairs to pack some of her clothes.

As she sat on her bed, her thoughts turned to the night of her seeing Sebastian for the second time in a long while wearing his brown tweed jacket and gold glasses. She took other classes at the London University King's College but she fell in love with the look of him and a mysterious air that he had about him. She watched on, as he would battle with his floppy brown hair in his eyes the majority of the time. That wide smile and calm exterior, his charming good looks and his intellect was undeniable, and she was drawn to him from the start.

She remembered just walking into his lectures, she wasn't registered with his class but she snook in and sat in the back. When the register was called she would laugh to herself feeling cheeky that she got away with sitting in his classes.

Bringing her thoughts back to the present, Rose put music on to calm her thoughts. Thinking of that night gave her butterflies that made her smile. Yet this feeling was foreign to her. There was a great understanding of each other which made her feel comfortable and confident she could trust him.

Being guided by instinct alone into the unknown was scary, yet exhilarating and Rose was beginning to enjoy the unexpected way things were turning out. She grabbed her diary and started writing in her diary.

FEEL

"From a dark past you must cast light, to cast light is to understand & to understand is to forgive. In the light of forgiveness comes faith and in faith brings the binding to the very meaning of life and to understand the meaning of life comes an impulse to love and to love there is the need to feel."

21

Walking up the grand steps of UCLA Berkley University he started to get a knot in his stomach. The principal met him at the front doors, shaking his hand and showed him in. He stopped briefly and turned to Sebastian.

"I hope you don't mind Sebastian but we are holding a Gala fundraiser for the London and LA University. It will be held here, we would like to present you with a lifetime achievement award and we've told folks that they can meet you, for a price of course, I would be grateful if you're there to pick your award up and greet your fans."

Sebastian looked taken aback but immediately replied, "Wow, well yes of course no problem I would be honoured, thank you so much."

The principal smiled and guided Sebastian to the lecture hall he opened the grand doors and Sebastian was in awe of how many seats there were and the vast space that echoed his voice around him. As the bell rang, the crowds of students began to file in.

The principal turned to Sebastian and told him to have a great lecture before shaking his hand, he left the room, greeting the students as they walked in.

Silence slowly falling around the room Sebastian began.

"Good afternoon everyone Thank you for joining me my name is Sebastian Lawrence and I will be taking you through your paces, I advise you take notes and all questions will be held till the end of the lecture."

The students looked pleased and eager to learn from such an academic professor, who had dedicated his life to his chosen field of study. Sebastian stepped up to the podium and raised the microphone slowly.

"In tonight's lecture I will be talking about Ascension. This word carries with it many   meanings; it resonates across time and culture; changing definition from place to place, era to era. For the Christians ascension was an act and a festival. The elevation of the Christ unto Heaven itself, celebrated then every year on the fortieth day after the supposed resurrection. For modern astronomers and ancient astrologers, it was used to denote the rising of some mystical star sign, or a mundane galaxy, over the horizon and into the night sky above us. Ascension became a goal for early aeronauts; the pioneers of flight, filling dangerous balloons with hydrogen or even hot air, to leave behind this mundane earth. To geologists, land ascends when volcano's spew forth, creating mountains out of nothing. Mountaineers ascended these highest peaks; and Emperors ascended to some gilded throne. And always, at its heart, is the idea of an improvement. An elevation. To rise, to soar, to improve. To become better in some way.

Within then the fields we study, philosophy and psychology, we find our species is drawn to this term. To ascend. To perfect oneself in some way. While differing cultures use differing terms- from Nirvana, or transcendence to salvation, at their core is a longing. A primal desire seemingly rooted in the very heart of our species, to ascend, something, to become perfected. Indeed, taken from this perspective, Ascension is in itself an inevitable part of the journey.

To exist is to ascend beyond what we were. Every step we take in a direction is further defining who we are and what we should be. It is psychological and emotional enhancement. However to evolve is to further refine, and that changes your very nature to become narrower. This is both positive and negative. The way people work together is through common cause and they conflict through differing ideas. It is like starting at the trunk of a tree. You choose a branch and follow it; you slowly get thinner and thinner as you pick a new path until you choose to come to a narrow point. That is when you are evolved to your very finest however, you have lessened yourself. The size of the branch you follow is representative of your diversity. Would you rather a garden of the perfect plant everywhere or a garden of incredible diversity.

Our diversity what defines us; a sociologist would call it our culture capital. People dream of us one day evolving into perfection. They believe this will make then into gods and they will be happy when that day comes. They are wrong. Say for example, that god is a being that ascended to godhood; I believe that this god dislikes things that are perfect. They are fundamentally flawed in that they are unlimited and unchanging. Our flaws are what make us exciting; a perfect being would create imperfect beings specifically because we are flawed. We are more interesting and far more vibrant for it. In that, we have already ascended, we are greater than god in the fact that we are far more diverse than it could ever be.

We can change, and alter where God cannot. If all people wanted was to be the equal of gods through evolution and indeed ascension, then they would be selling themselves short. We aspire to something that lessens us. We have already ascended.

However, regardless of how we may respond to said last statement, people, the general mass of humanity this is, seems to need a god to be omnipotent, omniscient, and omnipresent. This is an illusion construction by religions created thousands of years ago and is perhaps the primary purpose for the massive level of secularisation. Atheists seize upon many concepts and ideas to explain their decision. Perhaps the most common explanation is the concept of an all loving, and omnipotent god. They argue that god cannot be both all loving and all-powerful while there is evil in the world therefore he does not exist. Honestly, that being at least partially evil. It is not a justification for atheism, rather a very good repudiation of dogma. However, if you take this idea, and run with it, we find therefore God either isn't all powerful or isn't good, at least by our definitions of good, which are almost certainly different to the concept of good held by an eternal "perfect" being.

I would put quotations around perfect because the idea of perfect varies from person to person and so in order to be perfect this being would perhaps piss off a whole lot of people.

Perhaps be being its own definition of perfect or be eternally shifting and thus little more than a collection of energy that is never one thing and therefore doesn't have any of gods attributes. This leads us to the dangerous idea that humanity might be wrong about something.

This is dangerous because as a rule humanity tends to get very pissed off when they aren't right, and take a great deal to convince that they are wrong sometimes even when they are fundamentally proven wrong they refuse to believe it and instead continue to blindly believe what they have decided up to believe. A brilliant example of this is trying to tell a devout absolute creationist that that evolution is correct or that the real problem with debating with Creationists is simply non-Creationists do not realise you are literally speaking a foreign language to them. When you start pointing out the process of carbon dating rocks, say, or any one of the myriad scientific proofs that the world is considerably older than 6,500 years, they simply do not understand you. You might as well be speaking Greek. Why? Because their world view is so encased in their dogma, that they cannot comprehend a language that comes from anywhere but the Bible. They simply cannot. Many would say this is the definition of stupid. Or ignorant. But I ask you- who are the more ignorant? The Creationist who knows nothing beyond the language of the Bible?

Alternatively, the atheist who knows this fact and yet only talks about science, ignores the language of the person they are speaking to?

Let me ask you now- if some lost foreigner walked into this room and barely able to speak English he asked me to explain myself, and couldn't understand my explanations because his grasp of English was so poor, and my response was to turn to you and rolls my eyes and sigh and say 'He's doesn't understand what such and such means, isn't he stupid?'- would you think I am an intellectual? Or an arsehole? Yet time after time, this is what atheists do when encountering Creationists. Oh look how stupid they are, they say, never once realising that in doing so they prove that sure Creationists ARE stupid; but some atheists sure are arseholes about it.

All of which goes someway to explain why Creationists while they talk long and hard about the dangers of believing in evolution and engage in battles with atheists, actually fear above all things, Christians from more stable denominations. You see Christians who oppose Creationism speak the same language as them- they utilise scripture, the same Holy Book, the same words, all of which to show you can be a Christian and not a Creationist. Atheists may debate and occasionally make a Creationist change his views, usually predicated upon said Creationists own journey through education, but other Christians have been known to covert whole congregations away from Creationism. I mention all of this however, merely to illustrate not failings in debating with Creationist, but to draw attention to the underlying psychological truths- the model I see when people engage with Creationism, has been repeated through human civilisation. Humanity doesn't like to change. In addition, that which forces change is seen as a threat. And eventually people respond to threats, after the bluster, the veiled threats, and the real threats with violence. In some cases, they kill the person, just to be sure.

Now I am not suggesting some villainous conspiracy of Bronze Age priests, sat around some ziggurat and saying 'we should invent something to keep everyone obedient'. Religions are as old as the human race itself; whenever there has been a civilisation, from pre-Colombian America, through primitive Europe, through the great middle eastern civilisations that gave us the written word, through the Indus valley, all the way unto Chinas, in all times and in all cases, whenever humans come together, they unify. And the mortar that holds the bricks of said civilisations together is always religion. And with it, the idea of a God.

Except of course when they fell out with one another and by doing so made things all fall apart.

Now your assignment for this month is a minimum 10,000 piece on what your own opinion is and whether you would disagree or agree with me and why. Include a commentary if you like but know it will not add to your word count it may only be used for reference. I'll expect it in by the first of the next month. "

Now any questions?".... The room fell silent. Sebastian looked among the students and shook his head.

"Class dismissed."

Sebastian stood holding a glass of whisky out on his balcony overlooking LA in the mid afternoon sun. He felt happy; he was finally walking his course of life and had someone to walk beside him slowly being shown his frame of mind.

He walked to his guest room and took his top out of his bag that Rose wore the night before and he held it to his face. He breathed deep before putting the shirt on the bed. He stared down and around his surroundings. It was as though something was missing, something was deeply wrong. He felt a tightening in his chest and he dropped his whisky on the floor.

Kneeling down he hung his head and squeezed his eyes shut, flashing images of him on his mother's lap rocking back and forth, as she read to him being or nothingness a calm and serene feeling swept through him as he lay there listening to the heartbeat that belonged to his mother and the reverb of her voice as she spoke gently to him.

His breathing erratic he sat on the floor trying to get his bearings and focus.

He got up slowly and grabbed his phone he rang the flight path and asked if there was a red eye back to London that night. Luckily there was. He had to get rid of this lonely ache inside of him. Sebastian packed up fast there was nothing left in LA for him and his agent can wait he had the urge to be with her.

Back in London Rose got to Sebastian's house unpacked her things and sorted them in the guest room, she opened Sebastian's closet and took his shirt and pants out and dressed in them. She sat in his bed, pulled her knees up to her chin, and smelt his top.

She knew there was something different being with Sebastian it was a deep sense of having something she had craved for many years and had been pondering if it was even a real thing. To calm her thoughts she wrote in her diary.

PATIENCE

"He's as beautiful as a sunset. He leaves a cool warmth on my skin. The beauty sinks deep within my bones, I warm in his glow as he lowers onto me, I breathe deep and sigh hard. Only can a sunset leave you cold after it's gone. How I yearn for his rise, I look on time like an enemy, closing my eyes."

31

MUTUAL

When Sebastian landed in London it was dark and he quietly crept into the bedroom not wanting to wake Rose. He saw her wearing his clothes and wrapped in his duvet fast asleep. He lay next to her and after a full day of travelling he too was asleep within seconds.

The dawn broke and as Rose turned to face a sleeping Sebastian she shunted backwards nearly falling off the bed.

"You're back!" She shouted "I I ...."

Sebastian woke up quick from the shriek and sat up startled rubbing his eyes in a sleepy response.

"Yes I caught the red eye back and no doubt I have red eyes now waking so fast jeesh Rose your screech!"

As they both sat in bed, silence fell between them. Sebastian looked at Rose and Rose at Sebastian. They smiled and hugged each other as she kissed his neck, tears streamed from her eyes, she wiped them away quickly but Sebastian simply looked at her and smiled.

"I knew I had to come back."

They both lay down again facing each other fingers still entwined and their bodies close each fell silent intertwined into each other, both feeling an over whelming sense of peace.

Sebastian's phone went off and they each jumped, startled by the sudden noise. It was dark and he picked up his phone the light glaring in his face making him wince.

It was his agent. He answered the call as he shifted out of bed quietly.

"Hey sorry to call you so late, it was just to let you know that you have a break from everything for two weeks now."

Sebastian smiled at this information

"Thank you so much David for letting me know, can you send my new schedule through for me as soon as it's finished?"

"Yeah of course, have a great two weeks off buddy"

Rose woke up whilst Sebastian was still on the phone and got out of bed. She never liked listening to his conversations as she felt rude being there whilst he was on the phone she brushed her teeth and didn't realise they had slept nearly fifteen hrs she heard her stomach rumble and looked over at the mirror which had a time built into it and read 8.05 p.m. Sebastian ran towards her from behind.

"That was my agent saying I have time out between jobs and I'm wondering if you want to come to Morocco with me, just a breakaway really."

Rose couldn't believe her ears she smiled with her toothbrush still in her mouth and nodded madly with toothpaste splashing everywhere. He kissed her on her frothy mouth and they both giggled.

"We will go tomorrow so get packing, we're away for two weeks!"

"Oh my god for that long? I mean I haven't been away for that long before, I mean you're really going to get to know me, we have never spent that much time together, I mean, I fear you would…"

Sebastian gently gripped Rose's arms

"Shhhh rose stop please, don't over think, just enjoy the fact that you're away with me and you have time out."

She looked concerned.

"Well okay, I'll have to tell my clients that I can't freelance for them for two weeks as im also commissioned to do other work"

"Don't worry it'll all be fine"

Rose went to walk off but then quickly turned back with a look of curiosity on her face.

"Why have you never asked me about my job or my past or my family or any questions in general about me?" She asked wiping her mouth from the toothpaste.

 Sebastian frowned "Because your past is your *past*. It is exactly what it means, the past.

Your job does not define who you are and it does not matter to me if you are a lawyer or a plumber and your family well... They made you who you are but they're not you, I am only interested in what you have with me here and now."

Rose looked stunned. She knew where he was coming from because she had done the same thing, she had never asked about his past or his jobs because it never mattered to her. He was in that moment with her and nothing else defined that. She felt this feeling of complete satisfaction as she realised she had never been happier and in that moment that is what mattered. Sebastian grabbed her hand and kissed it.

"Your past made you who you are today there is no denying that and whatever you have been through be grateful of where you are now it could have been a lot worse same goes for me. I am forever grateful one thing I do is learn from my past to make a better now."

She smiled at him.

"Well about that, you never talk about your past"

He looked at her intensely,

"And I never will Rose, please drop it"

She looked shocked at his reaction.

Sebastian turned to Rose "they say that actions speak louder than words and with actions come feelings- let them guide you. They have done that for me and they have guided me to you..." he trailed off. "My past doesn't matter Rose".

Rose looked at Sebastian, she kissed his lips and he closed his eyes. This was a new concept to her she never refrained from saying I love you to anyone but this moment spoke volumes. Any other time any other person she would have said in this moment that she loved them but this didn't need those words. The sheer action in front of her was enough to know there was love between both of them this was unknown to her but it felt like it went on forever.

Sebastian looked up at her and kissed her gently on her lips. Her body aching her heart pounding she put her hand to her chest to calm her heart, Sebastian smiled.

"Be still my beating heart" he whispered, slowly tracing over her heart with his finger.

Rose felt she could fall to the floor as she had that exact same saying in her head the first time they saw each other at the party.

It became too much and she walked away a little. Sebastian walked over and hugged her. She buried her head into his chest and wept not of sadness but a feeling of home and of completeness. Sebastian lifted her head and wiped her tears away with his thumb.

"I'm sorry"

"Sorry for your joy?"

She laughed he handed her a tissue she cleaned her face up and Sebastian suggested they go for a meal because it was getting late and they still had to pack for Morocco

Ralf pulled up outside and they both jumped in hungry having slept for nearly fifteen hours.

When they arrived Sebastian took her hand and guided her in.

They both sat there saying very little but felt comfortable in silence sipping drinks and taking their time. They ordered food and it arrived quickly as it was so quiet.

Sebastian placed her hair behind her ears she shivered his touch was soft and unexpected.

"How come you have answers to all the questions I ask, you're never confused"

Sebastian laughed.

"Where there is a question there is always an answer! Whether we know it there and then or we have to research it we can always find an answer."

"Do you think there is a question that can't be answered though?"

"The question of life and why we're here. There have been theories about it but there is no truth and we may never find out." A faint smile appeared on both their faces.

Sebastian caught her look and mouthed the words *I know*.

They both smiled but their moment was broken by the server, who came over to take their plates.

"Would you like any desserts?"

"No thank you."

"Compliments to the chef the food was amazing."

The waitress smiled and nodded as she was picking their plates up and carefully balanced them on her arms.

"Thank you I'll pass it on."

Sebastian moved closer into Rose holding her hand and running his fingers over hers. He loved the feel of her skin, so soft, delicate and tanned. Rose always smelt amazing, and she tingled and adored the feeling of his skin on hers.

He kissed her ear and gently bit her lobe, she moaned quietly.

"Not here" she smiled

"I need to."

She felt her body give way a little if the earth was sand she would have sunk deep into it. She squirmed with sexual energy as he kissed her neck and breathed softly, tickling her ear

"Stop, I... I..."

"Okay I'll behave."

She looked at her watch and looked over the booth the staff were ready for closing.

"We had best get going they're packing up"

Sebastian got up and let Rose out, before fetching her coat for her and opening the door. They wished everyone farewell in the restaurant.

Whilst Ralf was sat outside waiting for them he was writing something down but when he saw them both he put away his pad and paper and opened the doors for them.

It was nearly eleven, they had not packed yet and their flight was leaving at nine in the morning.

"Goodbye rain and hello sun!" Sebastian said gleefully.

The car pulled up outside his apartment and as Ralf walked round to open the doors for them, Sebastian turned to Ralf.

"Be here or be square tomorrow," he chuckled to himself. Ralf looked at him with a confused look.

"Well Mr Lawrence where I'm from we say be there or be square"

"Where do you come from Ralf?"

"I originate from Russia but work brought me here many years ago so I have a full English accent."

"Well Ralf I relieve you of your services tonight and I shall see you tomorrow bright and early at 7.30am."

When Sebastian and Rose stepped into the lift he held her hands and gently caressed them so she could feel frustration building up there was no point getting started in the lift because before they knew it the doors flung open to a few people standing there waiting. They got to the apartment in an agonisingly slow time.

They started packing but Sebastian stopped and looked over to Rose he pulled out a box from the wardrobe and handed it over to her, she stared down at it and then looked at Sebastian. She opened it slowly and there in a gold box lay a dress no label to it but it was simply stunning. It was red and lace with a v line skirt and shoes to match.

"How did you know my favourite colour was red?" She wondered, awestruck by the beauty she held in her hands.

"You look like a red kind of girl," Sebastian grinned.

"My accessories gave it away didn't they?" she laughed.

Sebastian laughed, "you caught me red handed" he replied.

She laughed aloud, Sebastian looked stunned by her laugh as he had never heard her in such a way.

"I love your laugh it's unique, unique as in filthy but I adore it!"

"I hate my laugh" she scrunched her face up at the thought of it. Rose stood quiet, as she realised he had said love for the first time.

"Thank you for my dress Sebastian it's simply stunning you have good taste for a man" she held it to her body and twirled making the fabric swirl around her legs.

"Why thank you m' lady" and he bowed before her jokingly.

Rose went over and kissed Sebastian hard pulling away quick she knew that if the kiss lingered she would ravish him and they had a ton of packing to do.

They both got on with packing and finalising small details which things it felt like it went on forever. Rose finished first retiring to bed quickly. They had to be up early for their flight in the morning. Sebastian followed shortly spooning her and kissing her back, she pushed her buttocks into Sebastian so he thrusted forward gently. She could feel how hard he was her body was yearning for this moment but she knew there would be a better time for this, so she turned to Sebastian and stroked his face and kissing his cheek.

Sebastian snuggled her neck and they both fell asleep.

MORROCCO

The steward stood in the doorway of the plane looking at her watch and tapping her feet. She looked over to her pilot, who was also her husband and shrugged her shoulders shaking her head.

Meanwhile Sebastian woke up from a continuous buzz from his phone he looked shocked and sat up quickly checking his phone.

"SHIT SHIT SHIT"

"What are you okay are we okay?" Rose shot up rubbing her eyes slowly adjusting to both the light and to Sebastian's frantic tone.

"GET UP WE'RE LATE!"

"What?" She asked still half asleep.

"We're over an hr late"

"What happens now?"

"We run. Get your bags the flights sat on tarmac there's only a certain slot for us to go or we might end up waiting till tomorrow for air space!"

Rose flung herself out of bed and shot over to the wardrobe she threw on Sebastian's clothes, grabbed her bags, and launched them through to the living room. Sebastian telephoned the flight.

As Jen sat in the plane cockpit she felt her phone vibrate in her pocket; taking it out she stared at it and shook her head answering it.

"Hello you"

"Shit Jen I'm sorry we've just got up I'm so sorry we're just making our way out the door now!"

"Sebastian hurry your next slot is about to go how long are you going to be?" she stare at her watch.

"Thirty mins?"

"Your slot is going to be gone by the time you're here you have to wait twenty minutes for your next flight space"

"I'll take it, we're running now!"

He slammed the phone shut and he dragged the bags out of the door Rose was still hopping out the door trying to put her shoes on. They ran to the lift it was out of service.

"Oh god Rose we got to take the stairs!"

They both ran down

"Sebastian! Watch the rails they have been pain....ted."

Too late, Sebastian had already put his hand in paint.

"For crying out loud they're going to be pissed at me now!"

Rose stopped on the stairs creased over laughing; Sebastian was in front and looked up at her.

"It's not funny we're over an hour late I've got my hand in paint and I'm going to get shouted at by the hotel and the flight attendant."

Rose was doubled over she couldn't breathe for laughing. Tears were streaming down her cheeks and she was trying to grasp all her bags before they fell from her hands.

"Oh god Sebastian I can't breathe."

"Well save that for the flight let's go!"

Rose stifled her laugh and carried on running down the stairs. They got through the door and Ralf was stood there all the car doors open ready to throw stuff in and set off

Both out of breath Ralf put his foot down. Wiping the tears from her eyes Rose looked at Sebastian's hand.

"Jesus it dries quick it hurts"

"It's dried solid hasn't it…?"

Looking at his hand rose was failing to stifle her laughter.

Sebastian leant over and grabbed his phone. He rang the stewardess

"Hi sorry again we're just in the car but whilst you're waiting can you at all get some turps I've put my hand in paint"

Jen stifled a laugh

"Yes I'll get some now, see you soon."

They finally got to the airport Ralf did not have time to even open the doors.

Rose and Sebastian flung them open ran towards the flight desk but Sebastian stopped and stumbled back as he forgot the bags Rose ran on but Ralf waved them on to run, he carried the bags running behind them he got the trolley and left it by the side of them as they were checking in

"Okay you both have everything yes?"

"God thank you yes you're a star take the rest of the two weeks off paid enjoy yourself give my love to your family."

"Thank you so much Ralf"

"Have a safe flight and I'll see you both soon thank you."

Ralf jogged off looking happy for the paid time off.

They ran with their trolley to the baggage area and flung the bags on to the belt and ran through to the private jet ...There stood jen with a bottle of turps in one hand and some cloths in the other, Sebastian's long time stewardess and her husband both looking hot under the collar it was a glorious day. Out of breath, Sebastian musters a sentence.

"We're so sorry Jen." She stood shaking her head at him. He looked down and pulled a panicked face at her.

"Ummm okay yeah this is my girlfriend Rose."

Rose felt shy being called his girlfriend she felt about seventeen again.

"Nice to meet you would you prefer to be called Rose or Miss Banks?" she asked, checking Roses flight ticket.

"Rose, please" she half smiled.

Jen handed the turps over to Sebastian and they ran on settling into their seats they had to wait twenty minutes for the air to be cleared for take-off so the pilot James taxied the runway slowly.

Both slumped in their chairs Rose looked around the private jet, she had never been in one before it was small but comfortable all with cream leather interior the chairs were amazingly comfy and the pleasant smell of vanilla wafting through the cabin was beautiful.

She sat up and looked over to Sebastian who was scrubbing at his hands the sudden scent of beautiful vanilla soon jaded by the smell of turps!

"Sorry I know it stinks it's coming off though thankfully I'm dreading the tongue lashing I'll get off the hotel!"

Rose laughed, "you couldn't write our life."

"I think someone already has." He smiled.

Sebastian leant in kissing her and each time he did she closed her eyes his kisses were brief but soft and made her melt from the inside.

"Come with, I'll introduce you to the flight pilot a good friend of mine James, Jen is his wife."

Jen keyed in the code to the pilot pit and Sebastian walked in James turned round to shake Sebastian's hand

"So nice to see you, it's been a long time!"

"Yeah yeah it has, nice to see you too, I'd like you to meet my girlfriend Rose" Rose blushed.

"Lovely to meet you Rose, Sebastian's told me a lot about you."

"All good I hope"

James laughed "Yes yes of course!"

"Well nice to meet you James I'll leave you two to chat."

Sebastian kissed Rose on the cheek and she stepped out from the pit and sat back into her comfortable chair that hugged her like a welcome well needed. Jen came over with a bottle of champagne and a Malibu and coke.

"Thank you so much Jen"

"No problem, is there anything else I can get you both?"

"No thank you"

Jen was about to turn away but she turned back, and looked at Rose.

"Can I speak on a personal level?"

Oh god here we go a speech of how much she likes Sebastian and how she does not want me to hurt him, Rose thought

"Yes of course by all means" she replied putting on a big fake smile ready for the tongue lashing.

"I just wanted to say, I've never seen you so happy"

With a smile of concern, Rose frowned and thought *What did she mean seeing me so happy?* Jen then walked on whilst Rose sat there, confused. Sebastian came out from the pit and broke her thinking.

"We're about to take off"

He sat down, they both put their belts on, Jen took her position, and the captain spoke over the tannoy

"Welcome to flight 234 to Morocco we will be flying at an altitude of 40,000 feet and we will be approximately four hours flight time When we arrive in Marrakech it'll be 10.30 p.m and your chauffeur be awaiting on the tarmac when we land. Please put your seat belts on we're about to take off."

Sebastian looked at Rose, "You good with flying?"

Rose smirked. "Well I've never flown a private jet but I could try if the pilot passes out." Sebastian laughed.

The plane took off, he turned the TV on and turned the seats into sofas. They settled in for the flight and Jen brought food and drinks whilst Rose lay on Sebastian's lap. She couldn't believe her luck whilst lay there she pinched herself to see that it was all real Sebastian saw what she did he laughed.....

"Are you ok?"

"Yeah I'm fine I just feel lucky"

"It's not luck."

Rose smiled and carried on watching TV as Sebastian stroked her hair and caressed her neck. His fingers were light and silky to touch and sent waves of shivers down her spine. She could not have been happier, except for the slight whiff of turps!

49

PREQUEL TO BOTH MEETING FOR THE FIRST TIME IN THE LECTURE HALL A FEW YEARS BACK

Sebastian stood before hundred seats in London's Kings University that each stared blankly at him. He could hear the echoes of his breathing ricochet from the walls in the vast hall. He walked over to the podium, his hand quivering as he adjusted the microphone.

"One two, one two…" he said, his voice echoed & bounced around the room.

This was his first lecture trying to steer away from the acting scene. Doubts plagued his thoughts. His legs wanted to run far from the room but his heart and head rooted him to the ground he needed to get his thoughts out. He wanted to teach that people could think beyond the work of others and come to their own conclusion about life and death and everything that surrounds it. He felt sure that his views would be understood, but he wanted to learn more about himself and liked being challenged. Sebastian was more scared of the comebacks and critique he would have to endure but he knew that was part of him doing all of this.

The faint sound of the clock ticking in the background, Sebastian felt like time was mocking him. The countdown to what may be a complete and utter disaster, which will leave him licking his wounds. The bell rang suddenly and his heart pounded his hands clammy he gripped the side of the podium and swallowed hard.

"This is it," he mumbled to himself.

Looking up beyond the array of chair's he could see the doors creaking open and a slow trickle of students walked in looking down at Sebastian as they entered.

His heart jumped but he stood there smiling, pleasantly surprised that there was a large amount of students coming to his lecture.

OMNIPOTANCY

The stakes are high, he thought looking around the room that curved around his podium. All one hundred seats were filling up, echoes of student mumblings became deafening as everyone found their places.

After what felt like forever everyone settled and the noise slowly died down to a silence, now hundred faces staring back at him and possibly hundred questions to answer, but not before a few students walked out of his lecture he thought.

Standing there silent, Sebastian clapped his hands once, the sound echoed the room, the students jumped in their seats & laughter filled the room. Sebastian took a breath and began to speak.

"Welcome and thank you for joining me today, I am hoping to take you on a long and arduous journey of views opinions, theories, and philosophy all of which are based on religion, life and death. I do request that questions are to be asked at the end and you can make notes. I shall begin.

"Let us begin with the idea of an omnipotent, all power God. It is an excellent place to begin with, since for most of us, we all automatically picture in our minds our own version of such a thing, yes? One God. Monotheism. With the exception of any pagans or Hindu's in the room, it is an idea you were probably all raised with. One single all-powerful God." Sebastian smiled, allowing the words to hang in the air for a second.

"Oddly enough," he drawled, "The Bible does suggest that maybe God isn't a single being. After all does it not state at the very beginning- "Let us make humanity in our own image." That is a big thing- he says *our* own image not *my* own image. Of course, he could be speaking with the royal 'we' here. This is always a possibility."

The students start to laugh and Sebastian relaxed a little.

"However, if we decide to follow this word, which may, I accept, be nothing more than a translation error or linguistic style, but if we do, then surely it implies God isn't in fact, a single being, far more likely a congregation of deities. There is an ancient tradition that says the Jewish God is actually a composite of four separate Gods- Mother, Father, Son and Daughter, amalgamated into a single deity, the feminine aspect of which surviving today as 'The Holy Spirit'. True or not, it should make you think about what we mean when we say God. For many thousands of years for primitive cultures, God was feminine. After all- women are the creators and men are the destroyers."

He paused, focusing upon his notes, careful to slow down, not rush his points.

"Consider one of the many paradoxes of an omnipotent monotheistic creator God.

Literally, he is the Creator- creating everything out of nothing.

We have the whole field of science telling us you cannot make things out of nothing, but here is a figure that created the entire cosmos seemingly out of himself. This leads to conflict between believers in an omnipotent God and scientists but that misses the point. Why do we have to give him such powers? Why does the idea of God having limitations scare, well, all of us it seems? Why do we have to imagine God as all powerful? If he created the universe, say, if he is able to fashion this whole cosmos with all that is in it- and that was all he did and could do- surely that alone would be worthy of worship yes? If he could raise the dead, feed the hungry, cure the sick, but had limits to these powers- is that grounds to not consider him God? Why must we grant him omnipotence? Why must we demand omnipotence?" He took a deep breath.

"We have the Christian Bible- or technically the Jewish Talmud if we are being precise, and within it is the Book of Genesis.

We have the two versions of the Creation story, skilfully edited to appear as one, and revealing that God fashioned the stars in the heavens, by which we take it to be the entire rest of the universe yes, all in one day. And then spends the next five just focusing upon one little blue planet. This God is the indigo child- he just snaps his fingers and the universe just is. All the stars, the galaxies, the pulsars, the quasars; all the planets, all the singularities; all of it created in an instant.

"Then he comes to one tiny speck of this vast universe and shapes this little ball of rock beyond all other things. And makes oceans and plants and he must have spent a good twenty hours on the beetles. No, you might smile at that, but have you seen how many species of beetle there is? The sheer variety makes me wonder if God got kind of carried away with them." He raised an eyebrow.

"And then he is done. Six days in, he creates man and that's it. He rests. According to this- doing things like making the laws of thermodynamics, and gravity, and light and even time itself, this he can do in 24 hours and not break a sweat. But making a pig? Making daffodils?

And heaven help him, making a single male- this takes five days and tires him out? At this point I have to ask you- does this sound like an all-powerful god to you?"

Sebastian smiled at the students who gazed up at him, captivated by his every word.

"Or maybe it is just an allegorical tale after all- and maybe God created the universe and life itself via the methods known in science; that the cosmos began with a big bang, but he was there. That life evolved on Earth, but he was part of it; maybe when one group of our primitive ancestors became bonobos and chimpanzees and another group went off to become humans, maybe he was there, making that change. There is a creator God alright- but he doesn't seem very omnipotent now does he? He seems limited. Defined by the rules. Heck, maybe he is the very rules themselves. But again- he is not omnipotent?

"So why, do we ascribe this trait to God? Why do we seemingly need to grant God the ability to be all powerful? Is there some need within us?"

Sebastian waited, allowing his words to settle. It was a good introduction- the correct level of outrageous by academic standards, to keep his students interested. He looked around the room with pride- he had begun.

After the lecture a few students came over asking questions. Sebastian was happy with the results of his first lecture his nerves vanished leaving only passion in their place- a passion to share knowledge. The students sitting close to the front cleared the hall but remaining was one only student, Sebastian squinted, shielding his eyes from the projector.

"Hello?" his voice echoed around the now empty lecture hall.

"Hi"

"Can I help you?"

"Can you?" She responded in an inquisitive manner.

"Are there any questions you require answering?"

"Are there any questions you require from me?" Sebastian looked puzzled at this reply, a feeling he was not used to getting from his students.

"Excuse my forwardness but I didn't catch your name?"

"I am a student at this university."

"Well of course you are" he smiled.

"The question of life and death, Mr Lawrence?" she asked in an abrupt manner.

"Yes?"

"That is one of the main mysteries of life yes? That we have no clue what happens beyond life?"

"That is correct"

"Do you ever think Mr Lawrence that we are living a dream, and when we die we finally wake up?"

Sebastian stood back and sat down.

"You have a very good idea there miss…?"

"You don't need to know my name Mr Lawrence. I am exceptionally intrigued by your opinions but I feel somehow that they need further analysis to look beyond what is." She got up from her chair and Sebastian was looking down at his desk puzzled.

"What is your name?"

"My name doesn't define who I am Mr Lawrence I assume frustration will ensue but none the less, I will leave you with my thought."

After what felt like an hour, Sebastian got up from his chair and looked around the empty hall. He felt inadequate but who was that girl who had had such an effect on him? This combined with the nerves he had felt earlier gave him a migraine; he walked down to his podium collected his items and locked the hall doors.

As he turned round to walk away, he noticed the student down the hall.

He did not know whether to run after her or leave her, he had never felt this way before. A slow and crushing feeling began on his chest and he breathed deep and coughed harshly.

He looked at his watch to distract from the panic like feeling when he noticed it had stopped at six o'clock he knew it was later so tapped his watch and shook his wrist looking puzzled by it. He carried on walking to his car.

The next morning dawned, and the cold air hit his lungs as he stepped out of his house. He breathed in deep and smiled a flutter of feeling rose to his chest and the smile shot off his face and was replaced with a frown when he saw he was running late.

He got into his car and drove to the university; still half asleep he stepped into the hall, there sat one student in the higher tiers. With an impatient word he didn't look up and said.

"Hi, sorry my lecture doesn't start until 10 a.m."

"Time Mr Lawrence doesn't exist." Sebastian looked up beyond the array of chairs.

"Ahhh the student with no name." he smiled

"I have a name Mr Lawrence I choose not to use it"

"I'll ask again then, who are you?"

"I am, Mr Lawrence"

"So you're everything and everywhere are you?"

"I am everywhere I am everything indeed as we all are."

"What defines you?"

"Nothing"

"Ahhh" he began unpacking his briefcase slightly frustrated at the student who sat before him.

"Think what you like, that is the freedom of thought, but whether you're right or not Mr Lawrence is something to be left to the ego. What I do know is that the ego feels that it has the answer to life's questions we could live for eternity, on earth as it is in heaven, through a book that cannot be deciphered, called the Voynich manuscript but each time someone tries to decipher it, they lose their mind."

Sebastian looked up and frowned at the very words.

"Why are you choosing to tell me this specific thing? Why me? There are plenty of other professors in this university so why me?"

"Why not?

"That doesn't make sense, there has to be a reason…I mean you can't just turn up here and give me this speech about a script that lets you live forever once deciphered, I mean it makes no sense" Sebastian was growing more frustrated.

"You don't seem to like the unknown Mr Lawrence or death, something that doesn't make sense or something you can't control upsets you, frustrates you, so you want an immediate answer? To cure your curiosity…but you know what that did to a cat yes?"

"Yes yes curiosity killed it," he said impatiently, "but I'm not going to kill myself from curiosity!"

The girl smiled.

"Well that depends on what you're curious about Mr Lawrence you must be cautious of curiosity, sometimes it's best left."

Sebastian walked to the podium, turned on his microphone, and bent down to speak into it closely and quietly.

"Whoever you are…you're walking a dangerous tight rope with me. How do you think that you have me sussed?"

"I am a Behavioural Psychologist, and body language expert."

He raised his eyebrows shocked and spoke into the mic again.

"Then what are you doing in my class? If you're already a step ahead of it all"

She smiled coyly and replied, "curiosity"

He laughed.

"Ok, girl with no name our little lecture is over, come back at ten o'clock."

The student got up and started walking down the stairs. Sebastian looked on; he did not know what was happening.

"Will I see you in my lectures?" he asks inquisitively.

"You said that your lecture doesn't start for half an hour so I'm leaving until then."

"Is there any truth in what you've just said?"

"Is there any truth in anything Mr Lawrence?"

Sebastian was feeling frustrated, with a look of worry he shouted as she walked away.

"What is your name?"

She turned back and walked up to Sebastian, leant over to his left ear, and whispered.

"Rose"

She walked off and he smiled.

"Thank you" he shouted

Rose looked back.

"If that's even my real name." she smiled

Sebastian just shook his head in disbelief.

"Wait, Rose" Sebastian jogged towards her.

She stopped holding the books tight to her chest, her face flustered and her heart beating fast, her breath caught in her throat.

"Look, I'm wondering if you would like to meet for dinner and talk further, I am intrigued by you I won't deny that, so please do me the honour of joining me?"

Rose smiled and nodded, he heart pounding in her chest, she steadied her breathing and said, "Yes I'd like that."

Sebastian smiled and bit his lip.

"Good so say Thursday at eight I'll pick you up from your place?"

Rose looked at her watch briefly to hide her rising blush.

"Yes I'll drop you my address after class"

"Of course I'll see you soon" he turned and walked off with a grin on his face. Rose walked away with a spring in her step.

LECTURES

He walked back down to his podium and started setting up for his lectures; but he could not stop thinking about her.

He thought of her brown hair how it lay gently round her shoulders and bounced when she walked. Her brown eyes and her tanned skin that looked like caramel and oozed a natural beauty. He thought of how she spoke riddles and with no name that frustrated the hell out of him, making him feel inadequate with just a few simple words. Making his chest pound and his stomach churn and walking away from him in such a casual manner that wasn't rude or disrespectful, after thinking for a while, he actually didn't even need her name, he just found her magnetic.

Sebastian shot to the library to pick up a book about the Voynich manuscript, it held mystery that no one in the world could solve, this excited Sebastian and he could feel a course of energy flow through him and a quick smile graced his face replaced by a look of concern when he could feel his chest tighten again.

With his mind racing, he took the book out, somewhat determined to solve the mystery that possibly held a key to eternal life.

Sitting down and beginning to study the pages, his eyes flicked past each page with thoughts of the unknown language used, the plants that were drawn the horoscopes, and the naked drawings scattered about the pages. What looked like pools of water and plant residue, stained the pages showing how many others had tried to solve this mystery.

Before he knew it, the bell rang. He tucked the book into his brief case quickly and started his lecture when the hall was filled once again.

SEMINAR

The small body of students sat around his large desk. These were the good ones; the ones who pushed him, demanded more from him, argued back. In fact that is all they did. It was a weekly argument, a professor and seven students whose ideas clashed intellectually,, each undermining and strengthening each other. Some weeks, one or two would lead, other weeks, four or five would be clashing. It was invigorating. Sebastian was speaking, smiling at the passion of his students.

"So, you are saying I may be a bit wrong?"

The student opposite him almost laughed.

"I am saying you're completely wrong professor."

"Good," said Sebastian, "please proceed."

The student, Adrian, was half Dutch. A mop of blond hair sat uncomfortably on his shoulders and he always seemed to be on the verge of speaking. His mouth would hang slightly open, his face a mask of concentration. Today was no exception.

A few seconds passed and Sebastian quipped, "Adrian- the suspense is killing us."

Laughter sounded from the others.

"Fine. You contend that one of the more insidious aspects of religion is its imposition of morality upon people."

"No, I consider the ability of morality to shape people's views to be insidious. And to be precise the morality imposed upon society that takes sex as being somehow bad. As far as my experience goes, it's anything but bad. In fact I think it is universally accepted by all of humanity that sex is a good thing no?" More laughter coloured the room. They were in a playful mood.

Adrian nodded and continued "Alright, let me back this up a bit. The first issue I have with all of this, is that your view of morality is awfully limited professor."

"Wait? *My* view is limited?" Sebastian grinned, "This I've got to hear."

"You define morality as views concerning sex, or the seven deadly sins themselves. These are vices, and to condemn them is a moral point of view."

"I believe Adrian you will find this is how Christianity defines morality."

"Alright- but morality is more than just condemnation of vice. Morality is something inherent in all humans. No humans exist without moral points of view."

"Yes Adrian but I covered this in the lecture last week, morality is a by-product of every human in society. It is imposed upon humans by the society they belong to. If said society is religious, they take up that religions moral viewpoint. It's nurture winning over nature."

"But it doesn't work like that professor. We know its nature winning over nurture."

Sebastian blinked, "You are going to have to explain."

"Alright professor best to think of it this way; human beings, all humans, no matter where or when they were born, all of us are born with the ability to speak a language. It's in the basic synapses of the brain. It's like those children raised by feral dogs and wolves. Even if they have never encountered a human language before, they can communicate with the pack around them through grunts and animal noises. And whenever they are brought back to human society, they learn language fairly well. Humans are born with the inmate ability to communicate via language. Agreed?"

"Agreed."

"Now that genetic ability is the nature that- a new born baby will speak a language. What language they speak of course, will depend on where they are born. That's the nurture. So take a baby from China, whose parents and grandparents and great grandparents for countless generations have been Chinese and place them aged day one with a tribe on the Serengeti. That baby will grow up to speak Swahili not Mandarin. That's nature and nurture working hand in hand yes?"

Sebastian nodded his eyes narrowing.

"The same applies to morality. Humans are hard wired to be moral creatures no matter what. What that morality is depends upon where they grow up."

"How can you say they are hard wired?"

"Because they can feel emotions."

Sebastian sat very quiet. His eyes stared unblinking into the students, only allowing himself to nod, just once, to encourage him to continue.

"Morality and emotion go hand in hand. The first complex of morality we display is one displayed by all humans, everywhere. It's a universal one- which would prove it's hard wired into human beings yes? And it has an emotional base."

"What is it?" asked Susan, sitting forward, and a little concerned about Sebastian's mood, which seemed to have darkened.

"Disgust."

A few raised eyebrows but Adrian continued.

"Anyone who's ever been around a new born baby knows this one. When they are first about, the new born has literally zero issue taking a big dump in their nappy. None whatsoever. They are fine with it. And then one day, a few months in, they suddenly are not. They cry. They find it disgusting. Now maybe it's the sensation. Maybe it's the smell. But whatever the reason think about what that new-born is displaying. A complex moral judgement- disgust. Not just a simplistic 'I do not like this' but a visceral 'this is awful' response. They cry out. They have made a moral judgement."

Sebastian speaks, his voice narrowed, his eyes unblinking, "There are many who believe that this response is based upon the parents reaction. Grownups when they encounter baby poop then to look disgusted. The infant is merely taking the cues from their parents."

"And yet professor, every single experiment to prove this has failed. There is zero evidence that children pick up on cues from their parents, rather it's innate. And the implications are vast.

"Because," continued Adrian," it says that morality lives in the same part of the human brain as emotion. That it's a by-product of emotion. And if that is so, and given human beings are all emotions, then it would suggest that morality is not something imposed upon man by religion; but something man has already. Sure the nurture part will influence him, but based on that- I'd reverse what you said earlier Professor. Religion didn't get created and impose its moralities upon the humans in its culture. Humans gained moral thoughts and created religions to make sense of them."

Sebastian sat back and let out air- realising he had held his breath for some time. He spoke back to the young man sat before him.

"This is perhaps why so many through human history have longed for us to put emotions to one side; they get in the way of logic and clear thinking…"

Adrian, sensing something about Sebastian, a weakness perhaps, would not let up.

"No, not having that professor. That is the whole Mr Spock idea- that if you suppress all emotions you became this brilliant logical brain. That's bullshit. Know what we call folks with no emotions, or even reduced emotions? Sociopaths. They not right in the head. And the Spock example is so much bullshit anyway-for a creature supposedly in charge of his emotions; he makes loads of moral judgments all the time."

The students, even Rose had failed to notice that Sebastian was utterly still, utterly silent.

"When?" asked one of the others, intrigued at Adrian's comment.

"He shows obedience to the chain of command. Loyalty towards his ship mates. Bravery in the face of danger. Obedience, loyalty and bravery are morals. Indeed he serves in uniform- one has to ask is he showing bravery or valour?"

"Same thing," said a student sat at the back of the office.

"No they aren't. Anyone can be brave, but only soldiers can be valorous."

"How do you come to that?" asks another.

"The highest decoration in the British Army- the Victoria Cross. Given to the bravest of the brave right? Nope. It says what it's given for right across the top- For Valour. See? That's a separate morality for soldiers. Like duty. Like honour. In fact thinking about it- what morality does Spock show- valour, duty and honour, yes?"

Another student smiled- "Yeah- it's like our morality in our society says 'killing is wrong', but our soldiers would be useless if they did not kill the enemy."

"Multiple moralities all working together. See, society can cope with that. And humans can cope." The way I see it," said Adrian, "morality is something all humans are born with. It's part of us. We are intelligent creatures, and we assimilate complex moralities quickly because we assimilate complex emotions quickly. In fact the only people who can't seem to grasp morality are the ones who can't grasp emotion- the unstable, the crazies."

"Crazy is a harsh word," says one of the quieter girls and Adrian nods.

"My bad. You're correct- I will be precise. The only people who cannot deal with morality and emotion, which go hand in hand, are those whose basic psychological makeup is flawed from birth; some kind of misfiring in the brain. Sociopathy, psychopathy, extreme conditions, caused by the very nature of their brains themselves." Adrian paused and blinked.

"Professor, are you alright?"

Sebastian sits, his face a rictus of cold fury, his eyes far away.

"Professor…?"

He blinks, seemingly suddenly aware of the room around him. For a second his eyes lingered on Rose and he nods.

"I am fine. Sorry. Deep in thought. And not feeling too well."

He clears his throat.

"That's enough for today. Next week then?"

5 DATES IN

They sit, suspended in air, the lights of the city below twinkling in their neon glory. Rose tried to imagine how wide her eyes had been as they walked in.

"Well," she smiled, "you do know how to impress a girl."

Sebastian grins wolfishly and nods.

"I had hoped so. I figured a fifth date required something impressive."

Rose was trying not to look down. The view was enough to make her dizzy.

She had heard that in recent years they had revamped the walkways that ran over Tower Bridge, but she had no idea how far they had gone with it. Thick glass offered them both views of the river Thames facing north and before them sparkled London in all its nightly majesty. The real trick was the glass panels on the floor offering unrestricted views of the traffic pouring in and out of the City this evening. Rose grips her table a little.

"You alright?"

She smiled, "Yes. Just never expected them to put our seats on top of the glass."

Sebastian blinks and looks worried

"Do you want me to get a different table? Do you have a thing with heights?"

"No, it's fine," she replied, her eyes sparkling in the reflection from the candles, "it's just a bit much to take in. I never even imagined they would serve food up here let alone set up a restaurant."

"It's a pop up," he nodded, "only open for three nights. I had to move hell and high water to get us in."

The wine was chilled, the starters tasty and the conversation flowed. Rose watched him speak, watched the tiny expression changes on his face, listened to the excitement in his voice as he described the recent meetings.

"So, to cut a rather long story short- they said yes", he grinned triumphantly.

"Yes? As in 'yes we like your idea' or 'yes we want to meet again?"

Sebastian pops a morsel of food in his mouth and said, "Yes, as in we are bloody well going to turn your book into a TV series".

For the next twenty minutes, she rejoiced with him, congratulated him felt excited for him. She listened as he talked animatedly about the joint funding with BBC, NHK, CBS and other media companies with letters she had no idea where from. She listened as he talked of commissioning editors, about 'striding between popular and academic'. And about 'having a global outreach.'

Sebastian for his part was chatting away merrily, when he noticed she kept gripping the table every so often. This time her knuckles were white.

"It's bothering you isn't it?"

"What?"

"Sitting on glass. I'm sorry. I should have insisted…"

"No, no," her cheeks redden, "it's not that. Not just that."

She stopped and Sebastian blinks; "what?"

Rose sipped her wine and looked at him.

"Sorry. This is all a bit much for me. I'm not used to this. "

"Used to what?"

"All of this," she waves her hand vaguely, "I mean it's spectacular, like that last place you took me to, and like that box at the Opera, but I'm not used to this. I'm not from a rich family."

Sebastian's cheeks flush and he blinks hard.

"I'm not trying to make you feel bad…"

"I know, I know," she replied, shaking her head, "I shouldn't have said anything."

"No," he smiled, "it's good you did. You were blunt with me from the moment we met; I don't want you not to be that honest."

She sighed and a silence settles as their food is cleared. Sebastian poured another glass for him and looked at her; Rose nodded and he poured her one also, finishing the bottle. Carefully she lifted the glass, and gazed at it for a few moments before taking a big gulp. She placed it lightly on the table.

"I've noticed. You live for the now really, don't you?"

"How do you mean?"

"We have had what- five dates now? We talk about your work and the subject matter, which we both love, that's fine. And of course we have talked about your books and I am so happy this television series is coming about. But I don't really know you."

"Yes you do," he says, his face confused.

"No, I don't. I mean, I take it you have parents. Alive? Dead? You've never said anything about them…"

"Ah, sorry. I don't like to talk about my past,"

"That was my point. You don't like to and therefore you avoid it."

A silence returned and she watched, as Sebastian's face became a solid rictus of intensity, his eyes fixed upon the candle flame.

"And there it is," she sighed.

"What?"

"That face. Your fierce face. The face you make when you start thinking. I mean properly thinking. It's ferocious. A bit scary. And when you look like that you get trapped in that brilliant brain of yours."

"Sorry," he said, sitting up straight.

"You don't have to apologise. You've done nothing wrong. That's you. You think deep thoughts. This is a good thing," she smiles and gently touches his hand; "After all, when you think deep thoughts you write them down and speak them in lectures and publish them in books and those books are going to be this huge TV series. So don't stop doing it."

She smiles, but he sees her eyes and says quietly, "There is a 'but' in that statement. I can sense it".

"Look, you are doing it right. You are tall, intense, good looking, romantic, pretty rich and probably about to get much richer; you are incredibly smart and very attentive and someone like me could find herself falling for you. Falling very hard,"

Rose glances at her feet and smiles.

"It's just that… it's a long way down."

"You're not alone," he smiles, "I have to admit- I wasn't expecting to meet anyone either and I am nervous also."

"Why are you nervous?"

"Same reasons you are I suppose," he smiles.

"No," Rose replies sadly, "but that is my point. See I am nervous about falling for you because you are not all here. You have big walls up on your past; you have this huge life changing good news that means for at least the next six months you are going to be filming this amazing show; you are about to become kind of a celebrity. And your life is going to be filled with people and things and events and you will be so busy."

"Part of me doesn't want that. Part of me does- I mean what girl wouldn't dream of an amazing lifestyle like that.? But most of me would want you to open up. To let me in to that brain of yours. To let me past those walls," she sighs.

Sebastian sits quietly and finally says, "Why?"

"Because we all have walls, every single one of us. And I mostly want someone who will let me through theirs, so I will be comfortable letting them in to mine."

She finishes speaking as the waiter comes over. Declining dessert, they sit. A silence comes over them and rests on the table for a while.

Rose smiles, "So, now I have come across as some mad stalker lady, your emergency exits are here, here..."

He laughs, genuinely and smiles.

"No, you are not mad Rose. In fact you make sense. I could fall so deeply for you- this intense, infuriating, funny, demanding and beautiful young woman; I could literally give you my heart- but I think you're right. I think I'd be always holding back. And also, for the next few months, barely around. I don't..."

He stops and sips his wine, before carrying on.

"I don't want to be treated badly- no one does. But I also don't want to mess anyone else around. I don't want you here thinking I will open up just like that," he snaps his fingers, "Nor do I want to be some distant figure who's with you in body but not in mind."

They gaze at each other.

"I don't think we are ready yet to do this. You and me,"

She nods, eyes watering but no tears forming.

"Neither do I," she replies sadly.

"And part of me is screaming 'what are you doing' to myself," he smiles.

Rose nods and says "Being honest; and isn't that the best way to be?"

He nods. They talked a while longer, but it was over. As he hugged her on the footpath on the edge of Tower Bridge, he looked at her she stared back at him with sorrow in her heart.

Her breathing long and drawn he leans in to her ear and whispers "until next time".

Rose turns her face into his lips, feeling them sweep tenderly against her skin,

they feel soft and warm. She sighs, and closes her eyes, a tear form, he wipes the tear away.

"Rose, there will be a next time" he goes into kiss her softly but the cab pulls up and beeps his horn making Rose jump out of her skin,

The intensity between them both was palpable, she turned away and Sebastian let go of her hand. He watches her step into the cab and watched it drive into the sprawl of south London. He felt a wave of sadness sweep over him. He stood for a long time, before turning and raising a hand and hailing his own taxi home.

When Rose got home, she could not get the effect Sebastian had on her out of her head. She wrote in her diary to calm her rushing thoughts.

YOU.

I'm still feeling the effect of you on me even after thirty minutes has passed, your skin as soft as silk, your strength is impalpable and your smile hurls my fears aside.

Your hands I want on me, your hands through my hair, smoothing down my neck and your full lips against my soft tanned skin, your tongue to taste me.

Your energy to sink into mine, your breathing ragged your fingers lapping over me, the simple elegant sound of us.

Your voice brings me peace, as you whisper in my ear. I close my eyes in harmony to your words. The simple sight I see of you holds my attention, all else fades out.

Your words are with elegance that laces my body and thoughts, the feeling I graciously welcome.

When you are around me, I am a flutter where I once stood tall and strong your presence makes me weak and I stutter. My thoughts stop and I soften. When we look at each other, everything stops, suspended for a short while.

I fear too the feeling is weird, am I to regret any of this. I have not moved forward, I've stood still.

You make me want, you make me need, but only for you.

(Reverting back to PRESENT MOMENT place on flight to Morocco)

When they stepped off the flight the warm air hit them both.

Rose breathed in deep and held hands with Sebastian as they walked through the airport. They hopped into a cool air-conditioned car and were driven to the mansion it was only a short drive.

The car pulled up, Sebastian grasped the keys from his pocket whilst Rose looked around. She could hear nothing but the rustle of trees and the faint sound of the sea in the background.

"Finally here! The luggage will be here soon do you need a rest or are you okay?"

"I'm fine, you have an amazing house."

Amazed Rose looked around. The living room was gold filled with plush leather couches. The bathroom was a deep red with a shiny white bathtub sitting proudly in the middle of the floor. It was Moroccan themed with silk bed lining and a four-poster bed and the views of the Morocco Sea, on the balcony. The sea air smelt amazing. She threw herself on the bed whilst Sebastian walked in behind.

"You like?"

"God yes it looks amazing you have a stunning view"

"WE have a stunning view!"

Laying her gently on the bed and turning to Rose Sebastian kissed her shoulder. She smiled in delight as he pulled her closer to him kissing her hard on the lips her body ached her stomach flipped with joy. She quickly kicked her shoes off.

Kneeling between his legs she slowly parted them and began kissing his stomach. Teasingly lifting his top, she kissed up his torso slowly running her tong around his navel, breathing in his scent. She was in heaven, Sebastian moaned gripping the sheets and breathing in deep. They were interrupted once more by a firm knock on the front door.

Sebastian sat up sighing.

"Bloody luggage"

She laughed, "we just can't catch a break even when we're miles away from home."

"I know let me just get the luggage and then I promise that is it no more interruptions. Phones off, no one due around no house calls this is it final."

Rose smiled and looked relieved she stripped off and went to take a shower feeling grotty after such a long flight. Sebastian came back in the bedroom, saw where she was, and left her to it as he unpacked his things.

PASSION

Rose came out of the shower in the only towel she could find, that was two times too small. It only just covered her breasts and skimmed her bottom, revealing her long tanned limbs. Her hair dripping wet, she stood there in the door way looking at Sebastian. He held her gaze, breathing deeply and admired her body.

Biting his lip looking at her soaking wet hair dripping on to her pert breasts he noticed her nipples erected and her legs parted slightly. Rose was nervous, this was her first time but she had never felt as ready as she did this very moment.

He walked round the bed to admire her petite frame even closer. Her eyes closed as he gently grabbed her pulling her into his body kissing her collar bone.

He took his shirt off, feeling his body against hers. She was intoxicated in his scent and the warmth of his skin the ground felt like it was buckling under her. His touch was sensitive and soft. Unzipping his shorts he took them down, stepping out of them he picked Rose up and carried her onto the bed. She lay there breathing deeply as he knelt over her.

"God Rose you look…" his voice trailed off.

Rose put her hands over her face and giggled nervously but he took her hands gently away from her face.

"Don't be shy your body is amazing, you are amazing"

Rose bit her lip, her body aching for him. She had waited for this moment for so long.

Sebastian kissed her and she kissed back passionately. He left trails of kisses along her jaw line up to her mouth. Their breathing became exasperated and she took his briefs off.

"Wait."

"Are you okay?"

"Yes" Rose whispered back, her nerves turning to excitement.

She ran her fingers through his hair. He touched her in ways that made her feel alive with passion. They were intimate like never before and Rose had never felt so good.

Both out of breath they looked at one another and kissed softly Sebastian got up and took a quick shower and she lay there in utter bliss. She loved every moment. Rose wrapped herself up into the silk sheets and walked onto the balcony looking over the sea and feeling the sun on her skin.

Rose had been staring for some time out to sea thinking of all the things that had happened over the course of a month. She glanced at the clock in the room and noticed a faint sound of a piano coming from somewhere. Sebastian had gone from the bathroom.

She walked towards the sound of the piano what felt like a maze she found him at his black grand piano in the lounge. She stood in the door way with her head resting on the door frame listening and watching him play. She had forgotten that he had briefly mentioned in the past that he plays the piano and guitar.

Quietly she tip toed into the room and sat on a chair. Listening to him was soothing and relaxing he sounded amazing on the piano Rose rested her head in her palm and just watched. He looked up briefly from the piano and noticed her watching, he changed the tune he was playing with she sat up and leaned forward.

She was in awe of his talent.

As he finished the song she walked over, shuffling Sebastian to one side she sat with him.

"You're amazing on the piano!"

"It's what a year of practice does?"

"I played a little when I was younger."

"What made you decide to pick it up?"

"I don't know I thought one day it might come in handy, life's unpredictable!" Sebastian smiled.

Rose put her fingers to the keys and took a deep breath as she began to play. She took a quick look at Sebastian and played chop sticks, he half smirked at her whilst Rose laughed and assured him she was joking. Putting her serious face on she began to play, Sebastian looked on as she played and relaxed whilst watching her.

As Rose neared the ending of her song, Sebastian kissed her shoulder and she leant into his kiss

"You play incredibly well."

"I know! And only after 15 years practice!" She laughed aloud.

She looked over the room and saw he had a guitar, a banjo, and a few other instruments.

"I can play a tiny bit of guitar," Rose said but her stomach grumbled loudly before Sebastian could get the instrument down from its shelf.

"We will play that another night are you hungry?"

Yes," she blushed as he led her to the kitchen.

The two weeks passed in a complete blur of fun, sun, food and drink. Rose was loving every moment as she knew how rare and short these moments were in life so she breathed ate and felt every second she was with Sebastian.

She sat on the sun lounger reading her book listening to the waves of the sea and the croaks of the crickets. Sebastian came from behind her to give her a kiss, he had just come out of the shower. Smelling amazing, Rose breathed in his masculine scent and sighed. Sitting on her front lounger taking the book out of her hands he kissed her knees as Rose gazed at his naked body.

Putting her head back she ran her fingers through Sebastian's hair he kissed gently down her legs, to her feet kissing every toe individually then all the way back up her legs he stopped at her knees. Rose giggled and pulled the towel over them both as they continued.

PANIC-STRICKEN.

The final evening came and Rose was in the bathroom nervous as to how she looked as shown by the fact that she had been messing with her hair for the past twenty minutes.

"Up or down?" She muttered, pulling faces in the mirror of sexy or sultry moody or happy.

Putting the final touches to her makeup and carefully applying the dark sultry red lipstick to her lips, she thought of what would be next in their relationship. Trying to keep her pout as she applied the lipstick she could not help but smile about the thought of her future. However the smile was quickly replaced with a thought a nasty flash of her mother covered in blood holding someone, their face blurred… Rose shook her head to rid of the memory.

She stared back at the mirror and upon seeing her sad reflection; she nervously smiled back at herself. She was nervous as hell and hoped to make a big impression on him. She slipped on her dress, left her hair down ruffling it a bit and stood back in the mirror she bit her lip and barley recognised the confident sensuous woman staring back. She never could have imagined herself with Sebastian in Morocco in this stunning house. However, that is life unpredictable and predictable at the same time, Rose smiled at herself in the mirror and walked away guiding the trail of her dress behind her she put her shoes on from the bedroom and walked into the living room.

Sebastian stood by the fireplace sipping whisky; he looked over to see Rose stood there like a figure of beauty in her red hugging her curves. She looked nervous but feigned confidence.

"You look…"

He put his whisky down and walked over to Rose, she was too nervous to move and she did not know what he was going say or do; he came up to her, grabbed her hand and kissed it before kissing her neck.

"Je voudrais tout le dine sans rien te dire mais pour be rten dire les mots man quants tou jours alors alors, I would love to tell you everything without saying anything but to say nothing I still lack words."

Rose looked into his eyes.

"How stunning you look before me it is all I can do is admire you and feel what I feel which is just so amazingly happy and glad to be graced by your presence." He wanted to kiss her on the lips but he did not want to smudge her lipstick.

Rose was overwhelmed, she did not know what to say, but I guess there were no words to say they were happy in each other's presence, smiling nervously

"Sebastian you stun me by your sheer actions they speak louder than words, but can I just say how sexy you look tonight in your tuxedo!"

Sebastian smiled and shrugged. before adding, "well you know!"

They both laughed and Sebastian offered his arm out for Rose to be escorted to the car downstairs; where Ralf was waiting. He looked up to see Rose walk down, he stumped out his cigarette quickly and opened the car door for her. Ralf tipped his cap to her.

"Good evening Miss Banks, may I say you look lovely this evening"

Rose bowed slightly to Ralf and replied "why thank you for your kind words!"

Sebastian got in after her and she lay her head on him. Silence fell with just the sound of the other cars going past them she looks out of the window and remembers a time of peace and tranquillity with her mother, when she used to sit there listening to her play the piano.

She used to feel so at peace just watching her, as she watches on, her mother would stop and look over to Rose and smile.

All of a sudden, the piano lid snaps down on to her mother's fingers, she screams and Rose runs towards her but her mother screams for her to come any closer.

The lid opens and closes again her mother had moved her fingers, Rose watches on in utter disbelief of what she is witnessing. Her mother is shouting at the air for something to leave them alone, Rose looks around the room to what it could be, then suddenly her father appears in the door way and everything stops. Silence falls, Rose can still see her mother crying but no voice comes out.

She comes back to reality with a bump that the car went over. She was shaking, her skin was clammy and her breathing was erratic. She wiped her brow from the sweat and closed her eyes to quieten her thoughts. Sebastian interrupted her memory and made her jump.

"Are you okay rose?"

"I think I may be having a panic attack," Rose stammered through short breaths.

With concern, he made Ralf stop the car.

"Look at me rose"

"I can't Sebastian I can't focus"

"Okay let me focus for you listen to my voice, you mind is not here okay... I need to distract it, listen to me. Fact, no one knows who named earth, by the time you have finished saying I love you to someone, about 20,000 cells in your body will have died and been replaced with new cells…"

She looked at Sebastian with wide eyes her breathing beginning to calm.

"Oh…my…god….keep going" she gasps for air in between.

"Okay good, sunsets on mars are blue, on Uranus and Neptune it literally rains diamonds…"

"Oh wow," her breathing calmed and she rested her head between her legs. "I'm feeling okay, those facts are fascinating. How do you know how to do that?" She asked in an inquisitive manner from between her legs. But Sebastian did not reply.

"Did you have your mind on something else to make you panic in such a way?"

Rose looking confused

"No, what makes you think that?"

"When you are thinking of the past or future you are not in the present moment. And so when someone comes over to you and taps you on the shoulder you jump a mile it's because your mind is not present in the here and now and you are not aware of your current surroundings, it transports you to somewhere else."

Rose smiled, "Yes I was somewhere else, but it was peaceful and awful at the same time."

"Do you care to elaborate further?"

"No I'm sorry I do not."

"That's fine with me as long as you have a smile"

Sebastian raised her head gently to look at her

"Yes?"

"I don't want to talk about it Sebastian, it panics me"

"That's okay" he kissed her on the lips softly, Rose kept her eyes closed to embrace the kiss and feel the intensity of it.

They sat in the restaurant in a private section facing the Moroccan sea watching the sunset; little did Rose know Sebastian had a darker side to him about life.

"Where do you think we're going to go from here?"

"I don't care as long as I'm with you. I'm not making mistakes again I know I'm with you for life and I'm settled with you."

"Mistakes are not mistakes Rose, there are no mistakes in life only lessons to learn and move forward from ...trust yourself trust your instincts, that's what I did and look where I am now with you here?."

"But what if we never met again what if your instincts failed you?"

94

"There are no buts no what if's there are no failures, there is only now Rose here with you. Buts, what ifs and failures belong to the past or future they are here with us now"

This very moment and knowing where we are this very second where there are no problem's it's hard but with practice it will slowly sink in. You should also know to never take life too seriously."

"Is it going to be a long journey Sebastian?"

"You make life how you want it to be we're not here for long and as were passing through why not enjoy what we have now! It won't be long and arduous if you don't want it to be that's the freedom of it all."

Rose looked puzzled. She had only ever known rules, regulations, and never going outside the guidelines of anything, even putting rubbish in someone else's bin seemed wrong to her. She would not even go into a store and try on an expensive dress she could not afford just for fun. She only ever bought stuff she could afford she would never splurge. She kept a very wise eye on her money she never treated herself, never had a massage or spa days to relax, she would never jump a queue, never had a one night stand never did drugs or smoked or drank heavily. When her problems strained her she would go for a run and keep running till her legs could take no more. She punished herself a lot thinking she should know better when she told him this Sebastian could not believe what rose was saying!

"You're way too hard on yourself, everyone makes mistakes everyone breaches boundaries. You get people who jump queues and those who do not and that's okay. Do not take things too seriously, life is a playful thing. Each day I wake up Rose I count my stars I'm still alive, to see another day to see you to feel the wind in my hair the heat of the sun on my skin the drop of rain that free falls from the heavens onto my face, and to feel love for all of those things and for you.

"See I prefer to feel the sun and the rain and the wind rather than waking up and saying its miserable, it is too hot, or it's too windy I enjoy all the elements Mother Nature throws at us I believe there is a list of emotions you should feel at least once in your life: Passion, love, hurt and peace." Rose listened intently, he had such passion in his voice and as he spoke you could feel the love he felt for life.

"I want to feel like that I've felt, love but I have a heavy cloud over me I wake up and think another day another dollar, same day same way but since being with you my days have been better. I feel lighter in myself and the bad thoughts aren't so deep."

"It's good you're feeling better Rose, it will only get better as time goes on!"

Rose felt hopeful. She had faith in Sebastian as he spoke the truth in volumes and he gave her the confidence she needed for a brighter future. She bit her lip knowing tonight was the last night she would have with him for a while.

"I can see you thinking!"

"Yeah?"

"What is it?"

"I won't see you now for a while you're doing lectures I'll go back to work and I'll miss you so much."

"As will I with you but remember it's always nice to miss someone! It refreshes a relationship when you miss someone the heart grows fonder."

"I suppose so"… Rose's voice trailed off

Sebastian gently took her face, looked her in the eyes, and kissed her lightly on the lips; Rose cooed, she would definitely miss his lips.

They both decided to walk back to the villa the air was fragrant and the sound of the sea was soothing. The breeze was warm and they walked in a relaxed silence linking each other's arms whilst looking out over the sea.

Rose couldn't have been in a better place but the more she thought about how good she felt the more she feared death. Her logic was that if she had such a good life she would never want to die, but if her life was dull she wouldn't mind if nature took her away from the world. She knew if Sebastian knew she thought this, he wouldn't be happy. Or would he?

"Sebastian?" she said in a quiet tone.

"Yes"

"I've had a feeling for some time now and I know it's wrong."
Rose's voice trailed off

"Go on?" Replied Sebastian sounding intrigued.

"Since I've met you I've enjoyed my life a lot more I have felt love for you like never before and the more I feel love the more I fear death, I never want this feeling to end."

Sebastian hugged her close to him.

"Nature's cruel Rose we feel love for some things and some people but we see our loved ones pass and we watch ourselves grow old and eventually we die. That's something we can't avoid, but you're not alone in feeling this way, trust me.

Just enjoy what you have for the moment. You must admit defeat to nature but also you have to relinquish control of life."

Rose quietly repeated Sebastian's words.

"You can control to a certain extent like being careful crossing the road and looking after your health and keeping a healthy heart but ...

Rose interrupted impatiently, "Yes yes I get it! I get it but how can I give up control and let life take over?"

"Just enjoy life and don't over think, you'll get the hang of it soon enough! But this constant thought of death whilst you're having a good time is a reality check.

Let it encourage you to live life to the full and do more things rather then it been a hindrance. Just knowing you're in passing of this earth should make you more in love with life, just take your time with things and try not to over think.

"Just enjoy life with no over thinking.

Rose repeated this quietly to herself.

" For now take each day at a time."

"Thank you Sebastian!"

"For what?"

"Understanding."

"Remember I have been where you are now, in your mind it's a journey but it's worth its weight in gold."

Before they knew it, they were back at the apartment. They got through the door Sebastian slammed the door shut, which made Rose jump out of her skin. She turned to see Sebastian taking his tie off fast. Grabbing Rose around the waist he pulled her close to him, she felt her body tense with excitement. *So this was passion*, Rose thought.

Unzipping her dress quickly he threw it to the side, and she tugged his pants down, all the while kissing him hard, Sebastian threw her up against the cold wall, which made Rose wince, he took her away from the wall and lay her down on to the bed kissing her softly on her lips. He looked back and kicked the door shut...

The morning followed, Rose sat up in bed aching, hurting, exhausted but feeling amazing. Sebastian sat next to her. *Passion*, Rose thought. They looked at each other smiling.

Rose hobbled to the bedroom with cramp in her leg whilst Sebastian looked on laughing.

"Don't laugh it hurts"

"Sorry sorry I just had a vision of what you'll be like in fifty years time!"

"You think we will still be having sex at that age?"

"If I'm with you I'll be at it until I'm over a hundred"

"Here's to wishful thinking that even we last to a hundred years old."

"Well how about if we lived forever"

Rose shook her head, "I don't know what your fascination is with living forever, but be sure it will never happen." She closed the bathroom door on a frowning Sebastian.

HEAVY

Today was the last day together in Morocco, before she would retire back to her home and Sebastian would go about his work schedule. She remembered what Sebastian had said to her: to embrace the now. She looked over at the time it was 6.24 a.m.

"We'd better get packing we passed out last night without a thought to how much we have to do."

"No I don't want this moment to end."

Rose threw herself back onto the bed, "I know but we can't stop time!"

"Relinquish control," Sebastian laughed aloud and Rose smirked.

"Okay okay I get it ... Let's get packing the sooner we get this done the sooner we can see each other I'll be wishing the days away to just see you again!" Rose felt her heart swell and she raised her hand to her chest.

"I adore it when you do that, I know your heart it's deep and meaningful,"

Rose lowered her gaze and caught her breath, "let's just go."

The car parked up outside her house and Rose gazed out of the car window at her house. It felt so empty and lifeless it didn't feel like her home it felt like a stranger staring back at her. Sebastian grabbed her hand

"It'll go quick I promise"

"Don't make this harder than it already is Sebastian" Rose said as he kissed her hand and her face and lightly brushed her lips. She turned and got out of the car, he helped with her luggage and stood by her door watching as she grabbed her keys out of her purse and opened the door. It felt so strange it did not feel right she looked at Sebastian.

"You know you can stay at my apartment anytime Rose I know you have work so you must stay close to home but anytime."

"I know but it doesn't feel right without you with me."

"I'll be back before you know it and whenever I know I'm on TV I'll let you know so you don't forget what I look like!" Rose smiled at this thought.

"There we go I love your smile."

"Goodbye Sebastian."

They embraced in another long kiss before Sebastian turned away quick and got back into the car. He waved goodbye leaving Rose on the steps of her house. She watched as the car drove off. Rose took a deep breath looked into her hallway and dragged her luggage in. She shut the door and slid down it. Reality felt like it smacked her in the face wakening her up, she pinched herself

"Ouch I'm definitely not dreaming all that happened," she said aloud to the empty house. As she looked across the way there was a pile of letters in her door box she took them and sat down.

"Yep bills definitely back to reality!"

However, there was one envelope that looked elegant and pretty with handwriting that looked from the Tudor times she turned to the back there was a red-waxed stamp on it, it looked very official. She broke the seal and took out a bronze like ticket which read:

To Miss Banks this invite is for you to attend a relaxing spa day with us at the Hollow Rich grand house where you will pamper beyond

your wildest dreams Mr. Lawrence has set up an unlimited account on your behalf.

Rose was astonished. She hugged the invite and could not stop smiling! A list of treatments was on the back of the invite and she poured over what she could have...she could not believe it. Sebastian had heard her say she had never been to a spa she was grateful for such a thoughtful man! Rose jumped up from the settee and started to unpack. She put some music on whilst she unpacked and settled in again back at home.

Once unpacked Rose sat down to her diary, tired and dishevelled she began to put pen to paper.

Willow

"I close my eyes. I am encased in a cocoon of darkness. All I see are whips of my thoughts that have gathered lightly whirling in my mind like sand of the Sahara, I feel at peace. I feel my eye movements as I see my spectacle I have created, my mind smiles of the visions, dancing fading In and out, creating chaos with no theory.

I see the world blunt and raw but beauty Emanates from the earth and trees, the simple air I inhale is wondrous how I embrace that icy feeling that penetrates my lungs, blisters my soft skin, how I feel the wind in my hair every strand moving to the dance of the gusts.

On my face the rain is a wondrous feeling as it lands softly on my skin, explodes to drench me, the feeling is that of great and endless joy. The cold envelops me I feel it fall from me as it rolls lightly from my skin, it escapes elegantly free falling to the earth I stand on, and the ground consumes the drop as if being kissed for the first time.

I inhale the scent of Mother Nature. There is no other fragrance like it, the smell of rain after it has softened the earth I walk on, the grass after it has been cut the smell from blossom trees after they fall from there bosom of the branch. How life affects my senses, I take it all in with such wonder.

I wake up with such great fullness in my heart, the feeling I have another day to live, see, feel, and breathe the earth I live on, and my very soul is that of the world around me.

Anger is deemed as frustration with the world, the world feels nothing, we feel for it, my sadness fades into light, I feel but I don't react. Only with tears but not with fight, I cave into the light that consumes my very soul, I feel at peace. I am at happiness in the light and dark... Fear is that of feeling, there are so many words but only one feeling. We all fear. Fear reminds me all that there is ...that one day I will end I will free fall like a rain drop from the earth penetrating the soil I once stood on. The light I see fades the feelings will descend from my human, my bones will sow with the seeds of the ground.

I shall grow again, there I shall feel the rain on my skin, shade from the sun and beam when there is light shone on me, I shall cover lovers.

I will shelter, protect, move with the wind, my skin is that of brittle feel, but I live strong, I feel heat but I do not anger, I adore, I encase the feeling from within.

The rings show of my age and beauty, through the storm I bend and twist I flow with the rain and move to the wind.

Darkness encases me like a womb. However, I shall grow with the earth as the earth has grown with me. I weep like a willow.

BREAKING

Sebastian retired to his car and drove himself to the airport to board the plane to Hong Kong. Feeling exhausted and missing Rose terribly, he felt lost without her.

Closing his eyes for a fleeting moment his mind briefly flicked to a woman standing on the edge of a balcony with its bars broken and bent. Dressed in a red gown that flowed in the rough windy storm, he looked powerlessly on as he watched her fall from the balcony.

His eyes flicked open. He rubbed his face hard, placing his palms on his cheeks and breathed deep.

The plane came into landing, and he gathered his things and stepped off the plane, it felt warm he breathed the air in and walked through the airport to be greeted by Ralf.

"Are you okay Mr. Lawrence you seem a little bit puzzled?"

"Still tired and disoriented but I'm good Ralf. I guess I could be better but I'll see how I feel these coming weeks."

"Ahhhh" Ralf aired in an inquisitive manner.

Sebastian looked at Ralf in a very disgruntled way before asking what he meant.

"Nothing sir, nothing just curious"

"Well you know what you can do with your curiosity Ralf."

"Sorry Mr Lawrence" he walks ahead.

"Look I'm sorry, I'm just tired and I've got a long day ahead, and I wish to get home"

"So you're feeling homesick?" he said positively.

Sebastian looked to Ralf in a confused way, "Ralf what are you getting at?" he snapped.

"That you miss a certain someone?"

"Are you suggesting that I am missing Rose?" he frowned.

"Well yes Mr Lawrence? Do you feel that you miss her?" he looked on with glee.

Sebastian looked at Ralf and squinted his eyes, he straightened his jacket.

"This conversation is over" he abruptly stated.

With no words, Ralf put his head down knowing he had over stepped his mark, he speedily walked to the car door to open it for Sebastian and tipped his hat to him

Ralf got into the car and looked into the rear view mirror.

"I'm sorry Mr Lawrence I didn't mean to pry on how you feel"

"Ralf, leave how I feel to the professionals okay you know the score, don't push me."

Ralf nodded and started the car. Sebastian looked over to Ralf and touched his shoulder.

"Be careful what you wish for Ralf if you want it enough you'll get it, but sometimes all is not as it seems."

Ralf shook his head and drove Sebastian to his apartment.

Two weeks had passed and Rose had been to the spa, where she felt serenity and peace. Having her first massage was amazing but her mind was chattering away she couldn't silence herself but she loved the spa day and made a vow to do it more often.

Rose was getting on with work with a few occasions of drifting off into a daydream she was yearning for Sebastian and she pondered if he felt the same or if he was too busy to think about her.

She lay on her bed looking up to the ceiling her thoughts drifted off to her past.

Something she has feared for a long time she had not told Sebastian everything about herself, she had a secret.

It would expose her to a raw sense of feeling vulnerable but due to her past, she created armour. She had read so many books about how love penetrates armour it is all too cliché, she knew it would take more than love to break her free from the past. She needed to understand the reasons for what happened in the past. Rose curled up on her bed the good memories faded fast and she could feel her past consume her; she buried her head and wept. The music on the radio faded out, as did Rose to her thoughts.

I used to think there were such things as fate, destiny, reason and purpose; I couldn't believe we were just put here to feel what we feel see what we witness for no reason, Rose thought to herself. *But as my mother lay in bed slowly dying a death that she didn't care of my beliefs faded to just...doubt. I just now think we are here with no purpose or reason.*

But we are and that is a depressing thought.

I do believe to live a life you want you make it how you want it to be. I haven't made my purpose, I haven't created fate and I can't conjure up destiny or reason because it ends in disappointment, sadness heartache, and tears. This is the way I rule my life. I've had enough of that when I was younger. Now I'm twenty seven reality cuts deeper than the thought itself, that all we see and feel and create the purpose the fate and the destiny will mean nothing. All we will feel at the end of it is...nothing. Is there a man who asks us what we have learnt from life? I am truly not sure. We will never know until our time ends. Even that will be a surprise.

Life is cruel. You witness your youth and beauty and it decays before you ....Your mind deteriorates and we have no control over it. We go insane with no help from it, things are beyond our control and we have no other choice but to sit back and let reality just become our purpose whether we like it or not.

Humans come into this world with no request to have been born, and were made to live a life that is weird and wonderful then without request we die among our friends and family. A life we have created for ourselves. Life is cruel but it is how we handle it that matters.

To take your own life is a waste, but when someone gives up on life, life just carries on without them. Like a casino the odds are never in your favour you'll always walk away with less then what the house makes.

That is reality so either roll with the punches and enjoy what comes your way or bow out gracefully, but never end a life. It is a gift to feel.

My mum lay in a bed and I often think if there was a reason what would hers have been at that very second? None. She lay there waiting to die. Her body isn't ready to leave yet but she's serving no purpose. A waste of a life that can be lived by someone else who adores the way the world works. She angered me because she wasted her life. Giving up on life is never an option for me .I saw her do it. I would rather live it, feel, and die smiling with happiness...that I will no longer feel.

Do we live again? I will be sure to let you know as and when I go. But for now I live my life with love and lust, care and courage with my future daughter's heart in my hand.

Missing you.

Sebastian was in Hong Kong at a dinner party held by one of his friends he stood by the buffet area sipping a whisky drink in a room full of people. Despite this, he could not have felt any more alone, He watched as husbands and wives held hands and kissed and the looks they gave each other. He looked over the room and did a double take. A girl who looked Like Rose from the back walked into the room. His heart jumped to his throat but as she turned round, it was not her.

Sebastian get a grip you're in Hong Kong not London she won't have travelled all this way he thought to himself. He shook his head, took a big gulp of his drink, and left the party.

Rose had fallen asleep. Finally awoken by the birds outside, it had become morning, rubbing her face and stretching she looked at the time. She had not set the alarm and she was very late. She threw herself out of bed and into her clothes hopping through her bedroom doing three things at once; putting her pants on tying her hair up and putting her shoes on she grabbed her bag and shot out to university.

Rose stood outside her lecture her head feeling hazy. She was making mistakes on the notes and her thoughts were else where she hadn't slept well and was missing Sebastian she had hardly eaten anything and looking at her watch. Another week to go "Jesus wept how I am going to get through this"

The next twenty four hours seemed like a blur to Rose. She rolled back home after what felt like forever lazily stripped off and fell into bed. She turned the TV on and fell asleep.

She awoke again the next day...late. She threw her clothes on and ran to university forgetting to lock her door. She realised half way but couldn't be bothered turning back...She got into the lectures and was in a complete daze her face ashen from lack of food her hair a mess ....she cared very little.

As Rose was at university, she could not even be bothered to look up at the teachers, she just put her head down. The teacher's voice trailed off and an unusual silence fell.

Rose didn't raise her head until another voice billowed over the microphone, Rose raised her head so fast

"That's his voice"

His look of happiness turned to a frown of concern. Rose leapt out of her skin "SEBASTIAN" she shouted, "oh my god I didn't... I didn't..."

"I know I know my agent called and cancelled my lectures, I shot back here

on the earliest flight I could ...Rose you don't look good. "

As he said this she burst into tears...and quickly excused herself from her remaining lectures. Sebastian held her as she could barely walk she was fragile and hungry.

"Have you been eating?" He asked in an angry tone.

"No I've been in and out of university I've lost my appetite and I..."

"That's enough Rose let's get you back to our apartment you clearly need a shower food and a decent night's sleep!" Rose said nothing. She got in the car quietly and slid into Sebastian's arms and sobbed. Through her tears, she tried to speak

"I couldn't do it without you"

"Do what?"

"Sleep, eat, my thoughts the past it crept back in."

"I don't understand Rose is there something I'm missing? God forbid I was away for a full month would you even be here with me Rose!" His tone was Sharp and had unmistakable anger behind it.

"We will talk when we're home and you're showered and settled." Rose nodded and plunged her head into Sebastian's chest she shut her eyes. That familiar feeling of being home came back and she felt calm but she knew by Sebastian's reaction she could not be like this each time he went away.

They got home and Rose showered as Sebastian cooked her a full English breakfast and made her sit there and eat every bite. He kissed the top of her head

"Come to the living room when you're done and knew we can talk okay?" he said in a concerned tone. Rose nodded, but swallowed hard. She knew she had to face her fear about the past and talk to someone she loved from every core of her bones, but she feared he would not love her anymore. All the terrible scenarios we're going through her head.

She ate slowly, gathering her plate up and taking it to the sink she walked into the living room and Sebastian sat there with champagne and a dozen red Roses for her she smiled.

"Thank you Sebastian you're amazing and I love that you're back early I'm so sorry for breaking down on you."

"You have clearly been torturing yourself whilst I've been away and only your thoughts can do that so, what is it? If you're not ready to tell me now I will wait but I prefer for these demons to be told so I can help you."

"I know I've never told anyone of my past I know it doesn't matter now as I'm here safe with you but it's bringing it all into my happy moments and its bearing a weight on my thoughts and feelings. "

"Okay I'm listening go on."

"What you don't know is that I was tormented by mother, she was a spiritualist.

She had me and she seemed unhappy, she had suicide bids, my father, oh my god my father he absolutely adored her loved her inside and out but still. And I had to handle all of it alone so I created a coat of armour so I could fend off her drunken insults. She would ruin my artwork and destroy everything I ever created, she tore down my paintings and beat me some nights until I wept for her to stop. I had such a bad time with her I could not take any moments for granted. Just when I thought things were going smoothly and seeing the light at the end of a dark miserable lonely tunnel she would turn again and become too much.

After her cutting her wrists in front of me for the first time I'd had enough.

I got her taken elsewhere I was fostered out and I lived in London for a bit until I was older to move on. I had a few jobs on and off and become independent, I never knew why mum did these things to me, she was so jaded by her past she hindered everyone in her way and I vowed I would never be like her. Hence the no drinking no drugs no smoking thing. that's why I don't spend money on myself and enjoy life because I'm so afraid that if something good happens something bad will come along. I have lived with such consequences like that, that I can't enjoy my life..."

Rose's mind casted back to what she went through her mind broke over time and sudden flashbacks hit her like a rock.

Rose's psycosisc episode.

I read books like time did not exist. There are in fact, no numbers no letters, and we've codified our existence to make it more comprehensible. We have created the scale so that we can forget its unfathomable magnitude.

My eyes flick like lightening past pages my mind absorbs like a sponge, my reality is perceived consumed by the words I read. I melt away with my thoughts that fall from me, my belief now is unfathomable, there is no time, sleep is not an option, my imagination overwhelms me.

I gasp at the view that is played in my thoughts, my view I see of the world distorted by lack of sleep, the literature grips me and my memory runs riot

I sit up in bed staring into a void, I am at peace, this that I stare into is giving me my well needed answers, the now is all I have, my past cascades into darkness, I stare....have I breathed? I gasp for air not thinking...have I blinked? I close my eyes for a split second yes, I am fine. I feel nothing, my chaos has turned to calm, I rest in silence, my mind broken, and my thoughts have taken me.

My head falls to the books that surround me; the pen I have grasped in my left hand is taken by my right and placed onto the bed. My head raises from the depth below that I fell, I look around. Where am I? I look to the books and paper and I see a note..."I am you..You are me"...I look to my vessel...what is this I sit in? I feel my blood flow, the movement of my toes I stare at my flesh I move my fingers as if for the first time....I have regressed, I stare at the body I sit in. I know it's my body the movements are involuntary I smile...I feel happiness for the first time.

I brush the books and paper to one side the feeling is intense. The paper against my skin, the covers that sweep my legs, I go to stand. It's remarkable I stand I move, I walk, I feel everything the air I breath I actually breath I walk into a bathroom I take a cup, the feel of this is remarkable.

I touch the tap water elixir I fill the gauntlet and put this divine monstrosity to my lips, the liquid is beautiful. I feel every drip on my hand running down my arms, I look in utter amazement, the cold feeling, the water swarms my mouth its welcomed, my body thanks me, I swallow...wow I can swallow.

I feel the liquid fall inside me, I place the cup down and I look below, ah my body...clothes. I grab a robe, encase myself, as I turn I see a mirror, I look at my very being, whole top to bottom, I am divine, seeing me whole.

I open my robe to look, I feel shy, I giggle...I poke my flesh I view my eyes, I touch my face, I am in awe of what the world sees through me. I feel for the world and I am eternally grateful for this.

I close my robe and slowly walk down the stairs, were I feel I am departing from the mother ship to explore the world, I am...I feel hungry I look at a cereal box not understanding but knowing I must eat. But how am I doing this? Knowing what to do without knowing? I feel the items in my hands and eat it dry a texture unknown to me, the taste is taste...wow.

As I turn to the window I stumble back...earth. I am in awe of this earth, my garden to which I look upon. I swallow with no thought; step out from the door I opened and in amazement I am consumed by this planet. I feel for the first time all of this beauty. What is this I have on my skin? I cannot see it but it comes at me in waves, cold and then hot.

Ah wind, breeze my mind tells me.

I breathe in the exquisite aroma of nature. I look to the sky and the sky looks to me- I am. I walk to the floor and I feel the earth under my feet. I feel consumed by the ground walk with my palms open and outwards, I walk on the grass and my toes sink deep, I smile- I belong to this, I raise my head to the sky. *I belong to all of this.* A reflection to all that is in heaven as it is on earth. I am everything.

I stare at nature in utter awe with the way sunlight strikes the colours. I don't label as there are no names no separation on things it's all as one I just see the beauty that emanates from everything, I am everywhere. I fall to my knees and the dew encases my leg- what is this palpable feeling? Water fills my eyes stinging, my body shakes, a swell in my body, I blurt, putting my head in my hands, this is me. No name, no past, no future, I am here now this is all that exists for me.

My tears roll to my lips I taste myself I am divine I fall to my hands and I see the world for the first time in existence. I stand alone an ever expanding space, and planet that spins with such force I am grounded to walk the earth, nothing actually exists, I am to "create" we humans consider ourselves unique, so we rooted our whole theory of existence on our uniqueness. Time gives legitimacy to its existence, time is the only unit of measure it gives proof to the existence of matter.

I stand on soil nothing surrounds me, nothing…nothing…my thoughts ask me what proof I have of my existence? I have a mouth, a voice of which appears, I make noises but no sentences. My mind speaks for me, speaks to me. I smile...who am I? Wait... a question? This requires an answer?....a new layer unfolds in me...a playful concept I see light and dark, nothing fractures the days, nothing exists ....my head hurts...and I am back in my garden, a searing pain below and I touch between my legs, I gasp... what is this? Panic strikes- an awful feeling. I taste the liquid, *metal...ahh.* The earth of which I am made from, the colour is amazing. Is this what runs through me? My head burrows into the ground again... I am forced back to my first day on earth.

I stand alone, I am a girl...I let the blood trickle between my legs as I walk this amazing place with no name, I see myself as a child, my mind flashes back to black a void and then a bright light. *I was conceived...birth...* I touch my blood again. I am female...I conceive...I feel a gap to which I enter my fingers, what is this I feel...p*leasure*? I take my fingers away from myself quickly and stand shocked. I am to procreate on earth through pleasure but how? More questions fall into my thoughts like rain.

Rose blinked and she was back in front of Sebastian, her face solemn. He looked astonished.

ANSWERS.

"I'll admit it's a lot for you to take on especially on your own and losing a mother, where's your father in all of this?"

"When I was born my mum refused my dad access to see me, she was having an affair with a married man and his wife found out she wasn't too happy... Mum decided to end the relationship with him after his wife turned up on her doorstep and smashed a milk bottle over my head. I was only one year old but my father walked away from us both, mum was a mess.

He came back a few years ago when I was twenty he found me and we chatted for a while but he was weird, he did not seem interested in creating a father daughter relationship. He gave me money but that was it. I don't know what I wanted from him I'd been through the worst parts of my life without a dad, so I was too independent for a dad now, he was always asking about mum he's just so lonely at the moment I've lost contact with him I moved houses so much I couldn't settle."

"Ahhhh right ok and where is your mum?"

"I don't know I've lost contact with her too"

"Is that everything Rose? Your holding nothing else back? Im going to try and help you through this...What do you want from all of this?" His tone softened.

"A reason to why she did this to me."

Sebastian sat there silently, his chin resting on his hands. Rose took a sip of her wine. Silence fell and Rose had no idea what he was going to say. She had never shared this much with anyone. He turned to Rose and took her hand.

"We have your modern day spiritual guides now it's a very well-known thing we see it on TV in books and Internet. You have a support system to answers that your mum couldn't get a few years back She had no books like we have now she couldn't make sense of why her mum did the things she did to her, communication was restricted in those days. "

"Yes?" Rose sounded intrigued.

"Your mum did what she did because she didn't know what we know now about being in the moment, about being focused in the now this very second, no past no problems no worries. Your mum didn't have answers. She was consumed by her past and she casted that frustration on you. It wasn't personal it was her fight against herself and unfortunately you and her partners were caught in her personal cross fire.

It's a viscous circle of abuse and clearly you have broken that circle. You have the answer to what she needed many years ago and rather then you getting upset and frustrated wanting to know why you have the answers and help for you to understand everything of the past. It's a shame she didn't have the support and network we have now for people like your mum Rose but it was never personal it was her own battle."

She sat back in utter astonishment. It clicked. It all made perfect sense and Sebastian was right she was not able to forgive her for her abusive behaviour because she did not understand why it was happening and if you cannot understand something, you cannot forgive and move on.

"It all makes perfect sense mum always rambled on about how her parents abused her forced her to do things she never wanted and was neglected with lack of love and affection."

"It's a nasty cycle and it goes on for generations. Your mums mum would have never had the answers to her abuse either and so it goes on.

There's nothing you could have done so don't bother blaming yourself it'll be the first thing your thoughts do; knowing what you know now because you were in the same position as your mum minus the drink drugs and suicide bids. Yours was anger frustration and confusion."

"Yeah it was I couldn't make sense of it all but now it does my anger for her has turned to sadness I actually feel for her I was too busy thinking about myself how I was hurt and neglected but really we were both in it together and I never thought to how mum felt I never asked how she was or even showed any remorse. "

"You don't have to it's how you handle this information now that matters. Do you forgive your mum or carry on hating her? How do you prefer to feel?"

Sebastian got up and left her contemplating he knew it was a lot for Rose to take in.

"I'll leave you alone for a while ...." He walked off into the drawing room whilst Rose retired to the guest room, she needed time.

All these years she had hated her mother for wanting to end her life she had visions of even killing her. She despised her for what she did. She hindered her creative ways, her artist skills, Rose could never put pen to paper to start drawing without her mother's voice echoing in her head of how pointless she was and how bad her drawings were. Rose buried her head deep into the pillow but she heard Sebastian's voice echo of how it's a nasty circle and it wasn't personal she was projecting her past onto her daughter and Rose wondered,

If mum had known what I know now would she still behave the way she did with me?

That was a question that would never be answered and it was a bitter unknown answer she had to swallow.

She felt for her mother and the pain she had endured but she knew that when her mum met her dad she did see light at the end of a very long and dark tunnel. There was a glimmer of hope in her eyes, but when her mum answered the door to his wife, her mum's world shattered and there came the bitter cycle of violence again.

"Oh god" Rose spat and she broke into tears. Her body ached with sadness her heart was heavy and she gripped the pillow tight. She rocked herself to sleep. Sebastian stood outside listening to her. He knew this was going to be a hard journey for her anxiety and stress but little did he know she held such a dark secret. Sebastian left her alone, this was her breakthrough moment and she had to decide alone.

FINDINGS.

The morning was wet but sunny and the heat from the rising sun was quickly drying the damp pavements. With birds chirping Rose woke up heavy headed and stumbled to the bathroom. She raised her head to the mirror, putting her hands to her face feeling her skin rough and sullen.

"How on gods earth Rose" she whispered to herself. She shook her head and ran the taps until it was icy cold. Plunging her face into the ice cold water was refreshing and grabbing a towel to wipe her face she jumped out of her skin to see Sebastian standing behind her.

"Jesus Sebastian you scared me I didn't hear you come in!"

"How are you feeling?"

"Numb ...lucky I'm not in university today"

"I've brought you breakfast in bed"

"I am not up for eating."

"You have been through a lot you need energy sit and eat!"

She sat there eating her toast painfully slowly while Sebastian was tidying around her. Rose dropped her toast to the plate and broke into tears.

"Oh god Sebastian ...I forgive her I forgive her I forgive her." Rose kept repeating it sobbing through her tears choking on her toast Sebastian ran over to her and cradled her in his arms her body heavy, her sobs long and painful she wept hard her arms shaking. He stroked her hair rocking her back and forth gently.

"Rose it'll be fine don't worry you've got over the worst, I had to leave you to it last night it was your own personal journey that you had to go through alone to find your answer. It's not an easy answer either way."

Rose sobbed hard in his arms, "I need to find my mum I need to tell her but I do not even know if she is alive or not?"

"I can trace her if you give me her name and the last address she was is at".

"Hope, hope banks she was last in Manchester in a hostel." Rose gave all the information to Sebastian.

"Okay I will get on it ...when do you want to do this"?

"As soon as possible I need this out of me I need to move on. Thank you Sebastian how can I repay you."

"I've not even found her yet so hold your thanks."

"Not just for trying to find my mum but giving me the answers I have longed for I feel released like a massive burden off my shoulders I feel lighter today but with a heavy heart for hating her so much"

"You didn't know what you know now so don't beat yourself up over it your already too hard on yourself. Promise me you'll try something new each day it'll make times more exciting and wake up with a bounce in your step."

"Okay I promise"

"Right let me get on with this and I will get back to you, what do you want to do today?"

"Clean myself up? I look terrible! I might go for a walk around town too are you coming?"

"Let me get your request sorted and I will join you. This seems more important at the moment." Rose carried on eating her toast wiping the tears from her eyes as Sebastian walked off. She could hear him on his phone already.

"God he works quickly"

Rose had not seen her mother in years in about twenty years and she wondered what she looked like. Her nerves kicked in, what if her mother didn't want to see her or was still as angry as ever or was even dead. Her thoughts spiralled again, Rose clapped her hands.

"Stop Rose you're thinking too much." Her thoughts came to a sudden halt she ate her food quick and got ready. She felt like shopping might clear her mind and get her out of the house.

Ralf was waiting by the car for her now she had showered and put on some makeup she looked and felt slightly better in herself.

"Good morning Miss Banks" Ralf was happy to see her smiling and back to her bubbly self.

129

"Good morning Ralf can I go about town please"

"Of course."

Ralf pulled up to the town centre and Rose hopped out before closing the door.

"I won't be long Ralf do you want anything?

"No thank you Ms Banks.

She turned away and jogged over the main road.

Hours passed and Rose pondered the street, window shopping and grabbed a bite to eat. She didn't feel like buying anything but she liked people watching she took a seat by the river. It wasn't long before her phone rang- it was Sebastian.

130

AGONY.

"Rose! I've found her!"

"Who?" she snapped impatiently

"Your mum Rose your mum…"

"How?" Rose asked getting more confused by the second.

"Well simple really I rang hospital's around London, it was a wild guess because if she wasn't in London I would have looked further afield." Rose's heart skipped a beat and jumped into her throat. Her mouth dry like sand she grabbed a bag she had in her hand from lunch and threw up in it.

"Rose …Rose are you ok?" In a panicked tone, his phone pressed hard against his ear.

"Oh god I've just been sick" breathing heavily trying to wipe the tears from her eyes Rose asked "where is she?"

"She is in St Mary's hospital in London she's right here all along under our noses! But Rose she's in a bad way she suffered a brain haemorrhage, they're unsure of how long she has left." His voice dropped.

Rose felt like the world slowed down. She put her head in hands and dropped her phone to the ground. Slowly she looked down the road.

132

There stood St Mary's hospital the red bricked building loomed over her sending her shivers down her spine. Windows littered the front of the building, enticing Rose to go inside. Her hairs stood on end, faint prickles flowed through her body, as she made her way slowly to the hospital as if she was in daze.

Sebastian was still on the phone shouting for Rose, but with no reply he hung up. And rang Ralf to see where he dropped her off.

"Ralf its Sebastian where's Rose? Where did you drop her off?"

"She is down near central London" Ralf replied sounding concerned.

"Is she near St Mary's hospital?"

"Not far from there about twenty minutes away?"

"Shit, Ralf go look for her run now!" he shouted into the phone

"Is everything okay sir?" his voice raising.

"RALF JUST RUN TO HER! RUN TO ST MARYS HOSPITAL GO NOW! I am on my way" He bellowed down the phone to Ralf who was already jogging to his car to lock it and make a run towards the hospital. Sebastian grabbed his coat and ran to the car.

Rose stood outside St Mary's her mind was in a blur now that she was stood in front of the building that had her mother in. Did she forgive her Mother? Or did she still want to kill her? Her mind went blank and she walked slowly towards the reception area.

"Hello how can I help?" The nurse was finishing typing looking up from behind her glasses.

"My mum, Hope banks was admitted here I'm her daughter Rose Banks is she still here?" Rose asked speaking a low monotone.

"I'll take a look for you Miss banks, yes she's still here she is in a critical condition only two people at a time can visit is there only you seeing her now?"

"Yes ...which floor is she on?"

"On the critical ward fourth floor"

Rose turned slowly and walked towards the lift. She felt as if she was floating Completely detached from reality she pressed the button to the fourth floor but the lift doors opened and there stood Ralf out of breath and leaning down to catch his breath.

"Miss... Miss Banks, Sebastian told me to be here!"

Rose snapped out of her trance.

"Ralf what in God's name are you doing here? How did you know where to find me?"

"He was worried you were going to do something stupid!"

Rose laughed

"God what like? Smother my mother whilst she slept?"

"Well...yes" as he gripped the wall to keep balance from all the running, his lungs hurt and he had a stitch.

Rose's face dropped her tone became harsh and deep, "Ralf let me past I need to see her."

"Can't you wait until Sebastian's here?" He said in a nervous voice, almost whispering.

"RALF" she screeched "Time is precious! Every second I stand here talking to you I'm losing time with her!"

Ralf was shook to his core. He had never seen her like this. He slowly moved to one side.

Rose walked passed him keeping eye contact on him, she got to her mums door and stared through but her past made a quick rerun in her head the beatings, the swearing the spitting the hurtful comments the beatings the beatings the beatings over ran in her head.

She pushed the door open angrily but stopped and stood by the bed. Next to her she looked down and looking peaceful and calm lay her mother.

That's how Rose wanted to feel. She stroked her hair it was greying brittle and greasy. She touched her skin ....it felt warm and soft and wrinkly. She traced her mums face with her fingers she had never had a chance to hug her mother or even feel the touch of her skin. Rose tilted her head looking at her mums body she drew the covers back ...looking on her body was frail body, hid in covers of clothing, her toe nails yellow and bent and neglected her hands bony....Rose knew her mum had abused herself even more when she had left her.

Rose walked towards a cabinet where pillows were kept and grabbed one and walked back to the side of her mum. Rose stood there sobbing, with flash backs of her mother screaming at Rose and fighting off non-existent demons.

"I forgave you for a split second I truly did I felt your pain and it was horrendous it was agony but to inflict that on me, your only daughter because of your own problems." Rose gripped the pillow tighter.

"It's not going to help Rose" a soft toned voice came from behind her in the doorway.

Rose leapt in her spot dropping the pillow,

"Dad? What are you doing here?" Rose cried startled at the sudden apparition..

"I came to see Hope I've been keeping tabs on her. My wife is still keeping tabs on me. I was checking if she was going to get better checking if she was okay. You know she's missed you..." his voice trailed off and he sighed. "She regrets all she has ever done to you, it's all she ever spoke about"

"So even though she kept you away from me you still watched us from afar?

Do you forgive her?"

"Of course....I loved her ...she had a tortured past that was hard for her to come through.

Her mind kept getting the better of her, she spiralled and I found her in her flat having a fit that's when I found it was a brain haemorrhage she's been here for two weeks now.

Killing her will not solve all your problems! You forgave her Rose as you have just said. You forgave so don't let the past overwhelm you it's a circle and it's about to come round full pelt."

Sebastian came running up the stairs panting out of breath he stood there quietly listening to Rose talking, he turned to Ralf who was sat to the side with his head in his hands.

"How was she?!" He whispered.

Ralf slowly raising his head with red raw tired eyes and a faint voice replied, "She was scary, completely detached from reality like you said"

"Let it go Rose forgive yourself," her father continued.

She turned to her mum; Rose wiped her tears from her face and placed them on her mother's lips.

"I forgive you ...I truly do if it wasn't for the support by the side of me I would have helped you die faster...but I would have never forgiven myself I need to forgive by doing the right thing." She leant down and kissed her face, as she did her mum went into cardiac arrest. Rose looked up to the monitor and then at her mum with urgency. She looked behind her as the nurses raced in to resuscitate her, Sebastian grabbed Rose and forced her out of the room but Rose couldn't move from her spot.

Rose looked on in slow motion as her mum was being resuscitated everything stopped. Time, breathing, reality became a dream. The nurses stood away from her body each time they used the paddles on her. But with one final shock, the nurses stepped away and remained there…no one walked back over to her. Hopes chest lay motionless.

The doctor declared her death. Rose looked up at the time, 6.16p .m.

Rose fell to the floor and shut her eyes tight with tears that fell heavier than ever Sebastian knelt down and hugged her tightly.

The doctor came out, "Are you a relative?"

Sebastian looked up from Roses shoulder, "She's her daughter"

The doctor looked on at them both on the floor with a disappointed saddened look he responded.

"I'm sorry we did all we could…" putting his hand on her shoulder he squeezed it gently "I'm sorry, if you like please come and see me to discuss any questions you may have."

Rose closed her eyes tight and nods softly. Rose's dad rushed back in, gathered Hope in his arms and wept, hugging her hard. He rocked back and forth soothing himself with his love in his arms. He whispered delicately into her ear.

"We can be together, just find me and I will be there waiting, now and forever my love…peace has finally come." He buried his head into her chest.

Rose walked in slowly looking over her mother's body took deep breaths and wept harder than ever watching them both finally at peace. Sebastian grabbed her by the arms making her jump.

"Rose look at me you came here and you did what you needed to do.I've never seen it before but sometimes people hang on for that last moment to be forgiven I've heard about it so many times but never witnessed it until now, she held on for you Rose. She needed to hear from you that she was forgiven. She knew what she did was wrong and she beat herself up over her past and the things she did to you but her final breath was your forgiveness ...she heard you."

"I needed her to forgive me." Rose sobbed into Sebastian's shoulder.

Rose took one last look at her mum's lifeless body being held by her father, she shook her head as if it was a dream, wiped her tears and walked away.

"Look I'll sort everything out in the way of your mother's funeral…just be strong okay"

Rose looked beyond Sebastian with a blank expression tears still running over her face as she nodded in silence.

Ralf, Sebastian and Rose walked back to the car in silence. As they passed the nurses' station Sebastian stopped and talked to one of the receptionists, while Rose and Ralf walked on.

"I am sorry for before Ralf," Rose said looking pained, "I didn't mean to snap at you it was so out of character."

"Miss Banks please do not apologise you have had a very rough and emotional day...it has been for all of us."

He opened the car door for her, she flung herself in rested her head on the window and shut her eyes. Sebastian shortly came back, shuffled up to Rose, took her, and rested her head in his lap.

She raised her head to look to Sebastian and asked, "How did you know I might have done something stupid?"

Sebastian looked down at her and stroked her face, feeling the damp tears rough on her cheeks, "I was going to do the same thing a while back I wanted it all to end, and the only way was to end everything. I obviously didn't, but I knew straight away when I told you she was in hospital you might have spaced out."

"Jesus I'm so sorry today has been a weird day, I'm so exhausted." Sebastian stroked her hair soothingly.

"We are heading home now just rest on me okay?"

Rose nodded and before she put her head back down she looked up with a frown.

"Sebastian, where do we go? When we pass on is it peaceful?l Is it calm? Is it blissful? I mean... Have you ever thought that we are dreaming now and when we die, we wake up?"

Sebastian looked down and smiled at her. "This is something you have mentioned before at university when we first met...I'm glad you have mentioned this I have given it much thought." Sebastian paused for a second, his eyes glazing over as he searched the depth of his memory.

"Rose," he said gently, "There was once a nation of the most amazing people. They lived somewhere in Russian steppes- near the Black Sea. They were called the Khazars. They appear in history because they ruled, for a brief while, a vast Empire all across a vast part of the Earth- from the bands of the river Volga all the way south to Crimea and the Caucasus. They were this big thing 1200 years ago. Anyway, back in the 80's this Serbian writer created a fictional version of their history and in that book, he had a most tantalising idea. He suggested the Khazars believed that they were only half of their population. That they themselves were dreams of a sleeping race- and when they slept, they dreamt awake the sleepers who lived their lives."

Rose glanced over at Sebastian.

"It's an old idea. That reality may be a dream. Plato talks about it. The ancient Chinese talk about it- one Chinese philosopher fell asleep one night to have this amazing dream- in it he became a butterfly and lived a life free and flying. And then he woke and could not tell- had he just finished dreaming that he was a butterfly; or was he a butterfly now dreaming he was a Chinese philosopher?"

Rose smiled.

"You always get a bit silly when you're uncomfortable," she sighs.

He nodded slowly, "I don't believe we can come back. We should you see- you can't have up without down; you can't have white without black;

surely there must an opposite force to death; surely we must be able to return. Or at least we should have by now seen it. But the traffic only goes one way. No one ever returns. This is why I fear there is nothing."

Rose went silent for a moment, her eyes, tired and weary, gazing at nothing it seemed. Then she spoke in a quiet voice, "I remember a story I heard once: A bunch of dragonfly larvae live in a pond. They swim around together. They become friends. They speculate about the nature of their life. And of course the great larvae myth of the afterlife. They all know it. Supposedly, there exists a world beyond their pond- beyond the same rich waters in which they live. But they cannot imagine it. So they make a promise to themselves- the moment one of them dies, they will see, and if there is life beyond the pond, they will return and tell their friends.

"Time passes and lo and behold, one of them does evolve, and becomes a dragonfly. He suddenly discovers the world as we know it- the bright colours, the currents of the breeze, the vast vast expanse of the universe beyond the pond. Overjoyed he flies back, determined to tell his friends. Only he finds he cannot return. He is a dragonfly now- he cannot go back under water. All he can do is waiting for his friends below to evolve and join him."

"It's a nice story," says Sebastian.

"It was told to me to explain why those who died could not contact us."

Rose put her head into Sebastian's lap and began drifting off. Before long the car pulled up outside the apartment. Sebastian carried a sleeping Rose in his arms up the stairs and laid her in his bed. He covered her up and kissed her cheek, he turned back to Ralph who had followed him in.

"That will be all Ralf you have had enough chaos for one day go take the weekend off sorry for today."

"Please no don't apologise Mr Lawrence it's remarkable the breakthrough she's had it's unfortunate about her mother I'm sorry for her loss ...please give her my love when she wakes."

"I shall, thank you."

Sebastian walked into the kitchen and fell onto one of the seats on the breakfast bar. He put his head on the table and sighed, he looked up at the clock it was six. "oh god" he thought to himself *the clock must have stopped*

His appetite had gone and he hadn't looked at his phone for hours. He retrieved it from the table two missed calls ten text messages and one voicemail. He pushed it to one side and joined Rose in bed.

Watching her whilst she slept he smiled to himself, he knew she was over the worst of it now and it was all going to be a new start for her. and hopefully her demons would have been laid to rest, but he had to see the next few days.

RELIEF

Rose was woken up by the sound of tweeting birds and the smell of breakfast. She stretched out and looked to the window from where she lay it was a beautiful day and the sun was shining through the curtains. She noticed how she felt though.

Rose lay there feeling light. Nothing haunted her she had energy and felt like going for a run, Hopping out of bed she took a quick shower and got her jogging things out of her wardrobe. Putting on her running gear she noticed she had put weight on she frowned at her tummy and poked at her love handles.

With a sullen face she slowly walked into the kitchen where Sebastian was stood percolating coffee and putting the breakfast out

"Ah you're awake! How do you feel today?"

"Lighter in my head and my heart but I felt heavier in body-I've put weight on."

But I feel lighter in my head and heart."

"it's good that you feel better ...You're going running?"

"Yes it helps clear the cobwebs clear my head and gets my thoughts straight."

"Well you'll run off your so called weight then won't you? However, I don't find you've put weight on, you've hardly eaten over the last few days."

Sebastian placed the breakfast in front of her she pulled her face

"Eat your food will you especially if you're running you'll need your energy!"

"Okay okay"

Sebastian sat next to her eating his full English whilst she tucked into her croissant and coffee and wiped her mouth clean.

"Right I am off I will see you in a bit."

"Have a good run."

He got up and kissed Rose on the lips...she had forgotten how soft his lips were and how he made her all weak at the knees. His scent of sandalwood and musk wafted her way she breathed in deep and kissed him back harder, but pulled away quickly

"God Sebastian you see what you do to me you entice me".

Sebastian brushed her face lightly with his fingers.

"I've missed that smile"

"I know, I am sorry to put you through this I truly am and you have given me so much support more then I deserve".

"Love is endless I would walk the earth if it meant to be with you so this is nothing." Sebastian swallowed hard looking into Rose's eyes to see the reaction he had hoped for.

Rose felt a leap in her stomach and felt all warm she smiled at Sebastian and turned to leave.

I'll see you in a bit"

The door shut and Sebastian carried on eating his breakfast and started on his messages on his phone and voicemails, with a smile from Rose he knew he has said the right thing.

He made a start on his voicemails.

Jesus thought Sebastian *it's all come on all of a sudden I am going to be away for ages*

One of the places he had to go to was Cairo to do a lecture…

Rose put her headphones in, stretched, and began jogging. The music sank into her thoughts but they were not dark and sadistic, they were of remorse and sorrow.

Now her previous life had ended and a new one began, she could feel herself running faster she gathered speed going down a hill and round a corner. She hit the countryside the rural serenity soothed her. She thought of all the things she could do, like

trying that dress on that she could not afford or splurging out on herself when she didn't have the money. She could start the art work again she could buy foods she normally wouldn't buy and all this without her mother's voice in her head.

Rose felt free and she ran with a smile, a smile that turned into tears of happiness she stopped and leant up against a tree out of breath she sobbed, covered her salt ridden face and cried. This felt different. It was not tears of sadness but of happiness. She had never felt such freedom; she wiped away the tears and ran on. An hour passed and Rose came pelting through the door, knackered, hot and sweating, her body pulsated from the heat and she felt alive.

Seizing up she stretched out in the apartment,

"Good run?" asked Sebastian as he lay on the sofa watching TV.

"God yes"

She hobbled off to her shower. The cool water felt amazing on her sweaty skin. Putting her head back feeling the full pelt on her face she let out a loud sigh.

"Wow I forgot how amazing running is and how it makes me feel after"

Sebastian walked in to the bathroom "you talking to yourself?"

"Yup!"

Sebastian laughed.

"Rose?" asked Sebastian stretching out her name questionably.

"Yeeeeeees?" Rose replied mimicking his tone.

" I've had a few calls from my agent ...I have tonne of lectures and one of the places I have to go is Cairo and I'm wondering if you wanted to join me for it?"

Rose stopped cleaning her body and her jaw dropped shouting in excitement.

"Cairo Egypt, SEBASTIAN ARE YOU CRAZY.... YES PLEASE!" she screeched.

"Ohhh yeah ummmmm no can't do it I'd rather be at uni whilst you're travelling the world. Are you crazy? I've always wanted to do it since I was young! Of course, I will take a month off."

Sebastian looked at Rose's steaming body in the shower and he forced himself to look away.

"Just by being with me that's enough, I don't want thanks it's what we do when were as one Rose!"

She stepped out of the shower gave him a wet kiss before getting go back in. Sebastian did not want to take advantage of her he wanted to throw her up against the steaming glass and have his way but he respected that she was still going through the motions and would wait for her. Sebastian bit his fist and walked out whilst Rose looked at him confused.

It was Friday and Rose was in class. She took her final notes and the bell rang, she gathered her items and walked towards the exit.

"Hello Miss Banks, Sebastian has requested that I pick you up from here, he's at home waiting for you."

When they were finally home she walked into the living room and flung her bag over the dining room chair. Sebastian sat there with papers sprawled over the table and his head in his hands.

"We have a lot to go over...the itinerary is packed." He said in sullen tone.

Rose looked at Sebastian.

"We have two days before we leave we have not even started packing that comes first then you can go do your thing I will sun myself brown."

"Ummmmmm there's one more thing," Sebastian turned his back.

"Ummmmmm go on." Rose said in a light tone sounding intrigued.

He took a few boxes from behind and handed them over.

Rose looked shocked "no no wait, what is this for?"

"There is reason for this" in a worried tone Sebastian asked. "Will you walk the red carpet for a celebration gala with me?" He looked worried as the words fell from him.

"Oh my god seriously?" Rose opened her first box to find a dress made from dark red silk, she loved it immediately. Holding the dress against herself she danced around the room. Sebastian hadn't seen her so happy in weeks. She placed the dress down carefully onto the table and opened the next box,- it was a bracelet that was hand crafted to Sebastian's design the tree of life. He put it on her tiny delicate wrist and it fitted her perfectly, it was diamond encrusted.

"How did you know my wrist size? It fits like a glove it's so comfortable."

"Well whilst you slept…" Sebastian looked down as if in shame, and Rose began to smile.

"You measured my wrist" she laughed aloud "well I never" Rose said in a mock horror with a smirk across her. She gently opened the last box- it was a pair of shoes custom made to her size as she had wide feet.

"Don't tell me you measured my feet whilst I slept as well…"

"He looked down to the floor.

Rose could not stop laughing. It was all stunning but it was the funniest way anyone had ever had to get her measurements. She collected her items up and gently packed them away, her face was beaming. She placed her box on the table and gave Sebastian a hug. Her world could not have been happier as it was right there in that moment.

The Saturday morning sun pierced its way through the semi closed curtains whilst the room was filled with the aroma of fresh croissants. Rose woke up sniffing the air with her eyes still closed, she sat up breathed in deep and opened her eyes it was bliss. Stretching out she crawled out of her bed and sleepily made her way to the kitchen, ready to give Sebastian a big kiss but there stood a complete stranger.

"Oh shit"

She tied her dressing gown tight.

"Sorry I thought…"

"Hi sorry my names Ann, Sebastian's out at the moment, I didn't wake you did I?"

"Um yeah it was the amazing smell of fresh croissants" Rose replied with an excited expression on her face.

"Oh yes they're a secret recipe from my family"

She pushed the plate in front of Rose with fresh butter and homemade strawberry jam.

"Tuck in, Sebastian will be back soon."

"Did he say what he gone out for?"

"Sorry no, but I'm going now nice to meet you ..."she held out to hear a name.

"Rose"

"Rose a beautiful name I'll will see you again no doubt"

"Yes"

Ann shut the door and she tucked into her breakfast savouring every moment.

Silence fell. She looked around the apartment but the only thing she could hear was her own chewing. The day was clear bright day taking a deep breath she fell into the centre of grace, she felt balanced, calm and relaxed. Her mind silenced and she was finally at peace.

The apartment looked peaceful, seeing the dust settle in the sunlight she blew a little into the air watching the dust particles dance, and smiled.

"So this is how it feels to be free from thought. I feel playful."

Whilst sat there her mind stirred back to her and Sebastian. She had not been affectionate with him for a few days she felt a stir inside of her. *I feel like I need sex, I miss his touch his kisses his affection,* she thought.

She put her plate away and walked back to the bedroom, lying on the bed she unwrapped herself from her robe and lay there naked. She imagined Sebastian kissing every inch of her body, and as she did her fingers slid down to her clitoris. Her fingers guided round her hymen and she felt herself getting wetter. Tracing her dewy folds with her quivering fingers slowly gliding her fingers in and out of herself she could feel her body filling with an orgasm ready to explode. Hearing footsteps she looked over her knees, it was Sebastian.

"You couldn't wait? You're starting without me?"

Rose blushed and hid her head under the covers but Sebastian got under the covers following her underneath then he parted her legs.

"Can I help you?" Rose smiled nodding.

IN TIME.

The flight to Cairo sat on the tarmac with Jen and her husband waiting.

"I hope they're not late again," she said in a hopeful tone.

She heard running from inside the private runway, her face lit up with a smile it was Sebastian and Rose, panting out of breath.

"We're here not late" Rose looked at her watch "we're actually one minute early"

Jen laughed.

"Welcome to your flight to LA guys hop in were taking off soon"

Rose and Sebastian said their hello's to James as they were walking up the stairs and both settled into their seats ready for the long flight ahead. Jen came over with drinks and breakfast, whilst Sebastian and Rose looked relieved to have actually caught their flight on time. They tucked into their breakfast and set off.

"So we haven't had much time to talk since your mother's death, how are you feeling now?"

"Ummm good I'm still in shock with everything as it happened so quickly but time is easing it.

"Still fear death although you have seen it first hand?"

"I didn't for about a week, but then it creeps slowly back in, for example I sleep at night and a voice just whispers I will never eat breath see or feel again I just wake up in terror and I calm myself down, just simply saying that I must live my life to the full."

"Okay ….you'll get there; there will be one day where you never fear death this is your pinnacle of being in the now. Plus your over thinking distorts your view on life and makes it feel what was in the past rather then what you have now"

"I realise, that I do but it's hard! I've had twenty years of bad luck and when things are going my way I'm cautious of bad things happening.

It brings my happiness down and I think what is the point of being happy is if there is always something bad round the corner?"

"You can't keep thinking like that because that's life in general I know it's easier said than done but let it go. Do not over think, try for one day instead of thinking that is a lovely tree or bird, let that moment be. But if there is a situation that was awkward or strange or sad, then speak out. It's never the situation that's bad or sad or mad it's the thoughts about it that makes it that."

"But I always think people must think what I'm thinking like if there's an awkward moment I think everyone around me thinks it's an awkward moment."

"Get it into your head, not everyone is like you not everyone thinks like you. I mean if you wanted you could say something to break the ice but you'll soon find people have different thoughts and feelings far different from your own."

"I do over think, I do let the past get the better of me, it's all I know and when I'm in the now I feel lost as though I have no past I have no future it's just here and it suffocates me."

"Rose you rely heavily on the past to define who you are, but that tragedy and hurt isn't you now! You're mature, you're bright but you're not there with your mum now. Your entire situation has changed tenfold and I'm here with you every step of the way."

"Okay so I must stop over thinking and just feel more? If I am at all embarrassed, shamed, sad, mad or bad I must say so and not pent anything up? The situation is never how it seems it's my thought about it so if I change my range of thinking to positivity I'll react in more of a positive way?" Rose was revising out loud.

Sebastian smiled at how she was taking it all in. He continued, "there is no need to ever think negative, it gives bad results. Have you ever noticed a negative attitude get positive results? We were born on planet earth, but to beat the system you must understand it first. Everyone around that person becomes negative, but if you remain positive among negative people soon you'll see a change it'll take time but you will see a change."

"I need to stop being impatient as well…"

Sebastian laughed, "yes I think we all do."

Sebastian was looking at Jen getting angry and slamming a draw that would not shut. The hours flew by and it was soon time to land.

CELEBRATORY GALA.

Sebastian and Rose got ready at Sebastian's house for their night at the gala. As Rose stood in front of the mirror she looked to Sebastian with trepidation.

"Oh god I'm nervous I mean what do I say or do?"

"They will stop and ask you questions"

Silence fell.

"That's awkward!" Rose whispered but Sebastian heard her.

"Good, did you feel awkward then?"

"Completely!"

"How do you feel now that you have expressed the situation and not sat on the thought of it being?"

"Better it's not lingering on my mind"

"Feel the situation and speak out about how you feel. Words are there for a reason communication is key but the first thing you experience is….."

"How you feel about it?"

"Yes."

"This sounds so stupid, but in all my years I have never thought about speaking up in any situation I normally take the feeling home and let it stew or make my own assumptions about it, I've never discussed it or worked it out."

"There is a first time for everything"

"We're going off topic here, soooo will they ask me any questions?"

"Not sure some do some don't some will ask if this is your first time on the red carpet some will ask who you are but I'll introduce you first to clear the air."

Rose took a big gulp, her nerves kicked in and her stomach was doing somersaults. The night drew in and Ralf dropped Sebastian and Rose off at their hotel. She looked up over the towering buildings and felt dizzy.

"Wow the buildings are so amazing. How our minds work to come up with architecture likes this, it's simply stunning."

Sebastian took Rose's hand, "come on bewildered one I shall show you more of the dizzying heights of popularity tonight!"

Rose took a deep breath and walked up the stairs to the hotel. They entered the lobby and Rose was in awe. It was all gold and red with a massive check in desk designed like ying and yang it was beautiful, Rose could have cried she was becoming overwhelmed.

Sebastian looked over to Rose and asked if she was okay whilst giving her his handkerchief.

Rose wiped her tears.

"I'm fine I'm just emotional it's all just overwhelming in such an amazing place surrounded by beauty."

He squeezed Rose's hand gently to give reassurance whilst the bellhop took their luggage and showed them to their room.

"Here is your key Mr Lawrence any problems please call me I'm on all night as your personal assistant."

Sebastian looked stunned.

"You do this as a living?"

Leaning into look at his name tag, he saw his name was Samuel.

"Yes sir"

Sebastian again with a stunned expression asked "Samuel, a personal question I hope you don't mind me asking?"

"Please sir go ahead"

"Do you have a wife and children or do you live alone?"

"I have a wife with three children sir"

"Right"

Sebastian put his hand into his waist jacket pulled out $200.

"There Samuel tonight from me and Rose you can take the night off. Take your wife and kids somewhere amazing, don't live to work Samuel it's not what we're here for".

Handing the money to Samuel, he looked shocked and stood back fumbling his words.

"Sir...I...I...I cannot take this you're being too kind and I'm not sure management would be happy"

Sebastian laughed, "Samuel you'll make me and Rose happy, management shan't say a word I'll speak to them tomorrow, just take the money go home and relax. Do whatever makes you all happy."

Samuel slowly put his hand out took the money and bowed his head.

"Sir I have never received such kindness from anyone you have put my faith back into humanity thank you so much."

Samuel turned to leave, Sebastian almost forgot to ask. "One more thing before you leave, I do not want to see you until tomorrow afternoon please so no getting up early, say about midday?"

Samuel looked happier than ever

"Yes sir"

"Please call me Sebastian and this is my girlfriend Rose."

"Well thank you both and I shall see you both at midday tomorrow have a lovely night"

Rose looked on at Sebastian, "wow you're so generous you're amazing! I'm so proud to be with you"

"So is this going to be our word for the night …wow!"

"Yes it is because this whole journey up until now has been wow!"

Sebastian laughed and smiled at her, his smile suddenly turned to a frown as a weird sensation trickled through his body. He took her hand, kissed it and walked to the bathroom shutting the door and locking it.

He sat down on the bath side a strong sensation pouring through his body…he gripped his legs as they shook uncontrollably. Standing quick looking into the mirror, he gripped the sink so hard that his fingers turned white. Staring deep into himself he whispered.

"What is going on? What is this? Why do I feel strange?

A voice reverbs into his left ear, "keep asking questions"

Sebastian turned around quickly staring with fright at the bathroom door. His eyes begin to dart around the room; he looks quickly behind the shower curtain to see if anyone is there, seeing that no one was his heart beat harder, which turned to frustration. He then opened the medicine cabinet with such force he nearly broke the mirror. There were no meds to calm his nerves so, he closed the glass cabinet disappointingly. As he did he saw his father's face in the mirror behind him, his father's face white and ashen, hair so thin that it blows in Sebastian's tiniest of breaths. His father's eyes were so black and bleak it was almost a vision of an abyss, and a snag tooth that Sebastian would recognise from anywhere.

Sebastian fell back against the sink and his legs gave way beneath him hitting his head on the edge. Rose heard the commotion inside the bathroom and walked over with urgency

"Sebastian are you okay? It sounds like you're having a fit in there?"

With his head in his hands he shot a glance at the door but with his father's face gone.

He responded whispering to himself, "Something is happening in here but it certainly isn't a fit!"

"Sorry Seb what did you say?" She tried to open the door with frustration.

"Sorry I'm fine...I just can't find something." He shouted in a panic.

He muttered under his breath.

"I've lost my marbles that's what!"

Rose stands back from the door looking worried with a frown on her face

"Okay ill just be unpacking my things" hesitantly walked away from the door.

Sebastian took a deep breath and lifted himself from the floor; he washed his face and avoided looking in the mirror. He came out from the bathroom white with clammy skin and gripped Rose by the waist kissing her with a nervous look on his face, acting like everything was fine.

They stumbled walking backwards towards the bedroom, Rose's back hit the living room wall instead which winded Rose she winced in pain.

Sebastian picked Rose up in his arms and carried her through each rooms until they found the bedroom. Four rooms later they got there and he threw her on the bed. They both stripped off fast, Sebastian smelt under his arms pits and looked towards the bathroom.

"Quick shower? I don't smell too great care to join?"

Rose in a spiritedly manner,

"Yes!"

They both stepped in and the water fell onto their already sensitive skin, Sebastian grabbed Rose gently and bent her towards the shower window it steamed up the glass and they both moaned in enjoyment…after a while.

Rose carried on showering alone with a smile on her face and feeling fully satisfied as Sebastian got ready in the bedroom. She could smell the faint odour of his aftershave drifting through the door. She wanted to be taken again but there was no time as her nerves kicked in she jumped out of the shower and started to get ready.

"I'm just in the kitchen if you want me I'm three corridors down to your left turn right and take three steps to the left ….I'll be doing a snack for us both."

Rose laughed; the penthouse was like a maze and Sebastian's sarcastic tone always made her laugh. Rose stood in the bathroom wiping the steam from the mirror and looked at herself when all of a sudden there was a knock as the door. She wrapped a towel round her and she popped her head round the door.

"Because I adore you and time is precious I've hired a beautician and a hairdresser and a make-up artist to treat you like a princess."

Rose looked stunned.

"Noooo Sebastian oh my God thank you so much that takes a lot of weight off my shoulders thank you thank you!"

She threw the door open, hugged Sebastian so hard and kissed his cheek.

"Okay they're in the living room. You're having a pedicure, a manicure, your hair and make-up done and your dress is hanging in the bedroom."

Rose could have burst with excitement. She had never been treated so well. As she walked into the living room there stood three women. Rose's heart leaped with joy, and she jumped up and down clapping her hands with excitement, the women giggled at her.

"Right ladies I'll be in the music room if you need me, be gentle with her, she's my angel." Kissing Rose's cheek he left.

Rose sat on the plush comfortable chair and they began. She felt like royalty, the brush strokes on her face from the makeup were making her sleepy, the pedicure was relaxing and her nails were looking like a million dollars.

An hour and half flew by and the hairdresser showed her a mirror. There sat Rose: her gleaming nails, beautiful feet and her newly made up face, she looked in the mirror and did not recognise herself she could feel herself getting hot.

"Has someone got a fan or a bag to blow into?" The girls panicked and found a fan to cool her down. Rose's neck went red and her breathing became erratic.

"Should we get Mr Lawrence for you Miss Banks?" Asked one hairdresser seriously concerned. Rose tried to steady her breathing she could not talk, she felt like she was dying, her mind went blank her body felt weak. One of the beauticians ran off to get Sebastian he was at his piano playing when the beautician came running in.

"Mr Lawrence Miss Banks is having an attack of some sort of panic attack."

He stood from his piano and ran to her. Rose knelt down on the floor breathless and shaking and he turned to the women.

"Please can we have a moment I'll call you back in soon?" They walked out quick looking over their shoulders to see if she was okay.

Sebastian knelt down.

"Rose look at me, tell me Rose where are you?"

She was still breathless, so he ran and grabbed a bag from the kitchen.

"Rose look at me now calm your breathing lie down, look to me and listen to my voice...here are a few things you need to know. If you could swim as fast as Venus travels around the sun you could cross the entire Atlantic Ocean from NYC to UK in 2.5 minutes..."

Her breathing became calmer, her eyes darted back and forth, her mind could not comprehend such a truth.

"Rose with 63 moons Jupiter has the largest number of moons of any planet in our solar system and this shows how vast Jupiter is." He continued, seeing her breathing calm.

"Jupiter is so enormous you could fit 1321 Earths inside of it"

Rose sat up and asked "My god is that true? Seriously it's THAT large!"

Sebastian smiled, "hello, you're back with me, how are you feeling?"

Rose shook her head slowly, "I'm amazed, we're just these tiny ants living on such an immeasurable planet, but by the sounds of it the earth looks like a grain of sand compared to Jupiter."

He hugged Rose closer to his chest.

"You haven't even tried the dress on, you'll be unrecognisable." He said laughing.

"Rose, look you just panic, this is you, all you, you've growing to be a woman a beautiful stunning amazingly kind woman and I don't

166

deserve to have you in my life, you have given me more then I deserve and I thank you for that. Know who you are Rose, stop losing yourself."

Rose tried not to cry.

"I'm trying not to tear up so stop with your kind words or you'll smudge my make-up."

Sebastian looked into Rose's eyes and gently cupped her chin and asked, "Are you feeling better?"

Rose got up and looked around, "Yes let's do this thing!" She laughed.

Sebastian called the girls back in and he made his way back to the music room.

"Give me a shout when you're done you have 30mins."

They made a start on her dress there were over a hundred buttons from top to trail to fasten up and they had to straighten her dress and fan her trail out. They were apprehensive to give her the mirror again.

"It's Okay ladies I'll be fine"

Rose kicked her dress out and stood by the mantelpiece awaiting Sebastian to enter.

She was excited and her tummy flipped the girls stood back from her, greatly admiring her as one of the girls called for Sebastian. He walked into the room to see Rose stood in an elegant maroon dress her hair down and spiralled around her face. Rose turned her back a little for him to see the delicate details. He was speechless.

He stood there just staring at her then he broke his silence, "Ladies you have all done remarkably well thank you. That will be all."

The girls packed up their things and left Sebastian and Rose alone.

Sebastian walked over and held her hand.

"You Miss Banks are a vision of beauty, even if you stood in a bin bag you'd still stop me in my tracks. This is beyond anything I have witnessed I feel like the happiest guy on the planet right now!" He could not kiss Rose with her make-up on so he kissed along her arm. Rose melted inside and moaned

"Please stop I'm going to ravish you if you carry on and we have no time!"

He stood away from her and held his arm out, she linked him and then walked down to the car. He still could not stop staring at her.

Ralf stood outside with the car doors open and ready, he helped with the trail of the dress and in doing so told Rose.

"Miss Banks may I say you look exceptionally beautiful this evening." Rose bowed her head.

"Thank you Ralf it's very kind of you to say."

Sebastian squeezed in between the ruffles of her dress and she snuggled into his arms. Just breathing his scent made her feel comfortable and at home. The car circled the venue for a while until it was their time to walk down the carpet.

Sebastian turned to Rose, "Okay so there will be photographers all over shouting my name so I will be looking to them so they can take photos of me or both of us. They will either ask you to step aside so they can take single still photos of me or have both of us in the picture.

They will let us know but please don't take offence if they ask you to step aside it's all work."

Rose was taking deep breaths and the car stopped. Sebastian held Rose's hand as he stepped out, first helping Rose out of the car. Gracefully, she sorted her trail; the lights were bright and coming from every angle. She held her head high and walked arm in arm down the red carpet, it was busy with photographers shouting Sebastian's name and asking who he had with him. He never responded to the photographers shouting but he let them take photos of him and then both of them together.

Rose was in awe of everything that was going on around her, next to other celebrities her heart leaping into to her mouth. It was now time to be interviewed, Rose held Sebastian's hand so hard her knuckles turned white. He kept looking to her, giving her a reassuring nod and kisses on the cheek, they both stood in the interview area as questions flew one by one.

"How are you feeling tonight Sebastian?"

"Good, happy to be here tonight".

"And who is this you have here tonight?"

"This is my girlfriend Rose."

She stood there with her heart in her mouth smiling until they asked her something.

"So Rose how is your first time on the red carpet?"

"Daunting but I'm enjoying every moment"

She looked to Sebastian who winked at her.

There was a lot more, thirty minutes in and there were the same questions with the same responses Rose just wanted to sit down.

Sebastian ended the fifth interview as he could sense her body language.

"We need to get on sorry guys no more questions," he gripped Roses hand and kissed it. She smiled relieved that it was over. They both walked into the hall and took their seats, some of Sebastian's friends came over and said hello to them both and the lights began to dim in the room. Sebastian held Rose's hand again and stroked her fingers she felt a comfortable urge in her thighs.

She really wanted Sebastian, it was something about being in a darkened room and being naughty with no one noticing. The thought turned her on even more so she placed her hand over to his groin and started slowly stroking his crotch. Sebastian moved into her hand he whispered into her ear.

"God I want to take you here and now Rose Banks don't tempt me but, we will get thrown out."

He gently sucked and bit her ear and she slid down in her seat ready to melt away. The awards began and she took her hand away and lay it on Sebastian's lap they sat there and watched ceremony.

"And so, finally this evening we come to our guest of honour. This evening we gather to celebrate the extraordinary career of Professor Sebastian....I hardly think I need repeat the exceptional success he has had. Over the last few years it's been hard to miss his face on both British and American television; three bestselling books, the genuine excitement of 'Ascending'- a show no one could have predicted would have been a huge hit across the world. However, after all of that- he remains a lecturer. He still has students. Perhaps, we have to accept, that his fame means that we here at the University of London have to share him with UCLA Berkeley and the University of Hong Kong and elsewhere; but it's worth noting, rather than spend all his time in chat shows, Mr Lawrence has returned to academic full time a fact of which we are very grateful for."

The chancellor waved his hands.

"Enough, you did not come here to hear me speak- it is my honour to present Professor Sebastian Lawrence."

Sebastian looked to Rose with glee and kissed her. He walked to the podium shaking his head and, the room broke into loud claps and whistling. Everyone turned to watch him walk to the stage, as he walked up he shook hands and hugged his colleagues. Collecting the award, he thanked the chancellor and the room fell silent. He straightened his bow tie and with a nervous tone, he began:

"I would like to start by thanking my students, without whom I would be nothing, they teach me new things about myself each day, with intelligent arguments that make more and more sense as my life unfolds…" he paused and looked to Rose.

"I started with behavioural science, physiology, sociology, spiritualism, religion, I could go on and on with what I have studied over the years"

The audience laughed.

"I became a professor because I needed answers, answers that I couldn't get from myself, because I needed a different view from the outside…I needed a different outlook on life. Not just for now but also for the future, and the great thing is, life is unpredictable and random, and to understand it all and make sense of life I studied hard. We could harp on about everything in our lectures but that would be pointless unless we are willing to take those teachings and adapt them into our everyday live, to which I have done…or am doing."

Sebastian fell quiet and lowered his head, a sudden image of a gun to a blacked out head flashes up in his mind. He blinked quickly and shook his head, with a forced smile he looked up and raised his award.

"Again thank you it's appreciated"

Rose watched him leave the podium as the crowd clapped for him; he walked to the right of the theatre and into bathroom. Rose watched on concerned.

Sebastian slammed open the bathroom door almost falling into the room, he was alone, and he looked up to the mirror and stared into his face.

"Why can't you leave me alone?" he said gritting his teeth.

"I've gone this far without you, why now?"

He turned the tap on and washed his face with the cold water dripping off his skin, he looked up and saw blood dripping from his face.

He looked down to the sink and there is blood pouring from the taps. He moved to the next sink and ran the tap and it comes out clear he washed his face furiously. The water cascading down over the floor he looked up to see his face dripping with water. He sighed with relief and closed his eyes tight.

"I will not do this," he whispered to himself.

Grabbing a towel he wiped his face and hands and walked from the bathroom.

He joined Rose as she held out her hand for Sebastian to take, he could hear Rose's stomach rumbling.

"We're going to get something to eat now it's a buffet with the most amazing food you'll ever try." Forcing a smile. Sebastian led her to the buffet table.

Rose liked trying new things; and there lay a buffet fit for a king, every kind of food you could think of. It stretched around the ballroom and Rose's pupils dilated.

173

"Where do I begin?" she smiled and looked over to Sebastian, but he was staring blankly into thin air.

"I'm not sure let's start from one end to the other," he said with a vague expression

Rose smiled, "Good idea"

After making their way round the buffet twice the only thing Rose had not tried was caviar. She took a little on a cracker and smelt it, then took a bite. Sebastian looked at her as she took a bite and her face turned sour with a mouth full.

"Quick get a tissue," she said in a panicked tone.

Sebastian laughed and got a serviette for her and she spat it out, her mouth all still black.

Sebastian was in stitches, she had broken him out of his trance.

"Can we go home please I need to rinse my mouth out?"

"I think it's an acquired taste," he said trying to conceal his laugh.

They walked to the car Ralf waiting he frowned at Rose's face

"Something not agreed with you?" He asked with curiosity.

Rose pulled her tongue out

"No it didn't Ralf, caviar is not to my taste"

"Oh dear" he laughed to himself as he opened the car door. They both jumped in, she leaned her head on Sebastian

"Thank you for an amazing night I'm stuffed as a camel and I'm ready to relax!"

"As am I."

Sebastian stroked her hair entwining strands of it between his fingers until Rose fell asleep.

After a long car ride they were finally at the hotel, Sebastian carried Rose into the bedroom and delicately placed her onto the bed. He stood back and watched as she slept in her gown.

She looks like a picture of heaven, Sebastian thought.

He paused to take the moment in as he had never known such beauty in human form.

Sebastian stripped off and crept to the piano room.

The room was pitch-black dark when Rose awoke to the sound of a piano. She looked at her clock it was 3am. Still wearing her dress she snuggled her face into it's ruffles smelling a mix of her perfume, Sebastian's cologne… and caviar.

I never want to take it off, she thought to herself.

She got up and walked towards the sound of the piano. She had no idea of where it was coming from. The house, being a maze, led her to the kitchen, the bathroom, the dining room. Becoming impatient she called his name.

"I can hear you but I can't see where you are what room are you in?"

The piano stopped playing. She heard footsteps coming from afar and, behind her a soft kiss landed on her shoulder, Rose jumped out of her skin.

She went to turn but Sebastian stopped her abruptly, "don't turn around."

Feeling his breath on her ear made her weak.

"Okay" she whispered.

He kissed gently round her shoulders, stroked her hair to the side. Kissing up her neck and stroking her shoulders, she put her head to one side; he licked her neck slowly sucked on her ear lobe. He slipped off her straps from the dress

"I need you."

Rose could have melted into the ground, he began unbuttoning her dress one by one and with each button was undone he kissed her back.

"You know there are hundred buttons on this dress!"

Rose turned her head

"Don't move" he growled as he carried on kissing her.

"You're worth more than one hundred kisses".

176

She smiled and just enjoyed the moment; the dress fell away from her body and dropped round her feet softly.

Sebastian knelt down he slowly parted her legs kissing up her inner thighs Rose moaned she could feel her legs shaking, as each of his kisses got higher she got weaker.

"Stay standing." He whispered from below.

"I'm trying" she gasped, as he picked her up and headed towards the bedroom...

It was there last day in LA and Rose peered out of the window of the car as it was taking them back to the airport for Sebastian's next round of lectures.

"Cairo here we come!" Rose said in an excited tone. "I've always wanted to go there but never alone its beautiful, an absolute paradise." She clapped her hands in excitement, Sebastian smiled.

"Well if you think Cairo is paradise you should see the hotel we're going to!"

Rose's eyes widened as far they could go and she slowly turned to Sebastian and gripped his hand hard shaking him he took her hand and made an excited expression on his face!

"Its not a six star hotel Rose"

Rose slumped down on her chair

"I'm so embarrassed"

"Don't be you weren't to know, I don't want to spend a fortune on a £900 a night hotel Rose. As long as I have you here I could sleep on the beach and be just as happy.

Rose smiled and kissed Sebastian on the cheek lightly resting her head on him.

The next day, after flying for hours they finally landed at Cairo airport, Rose's face gleamed as she passed through the huge building with beautiful architecture stretching among the vast space of the building. Chrome shone out bright from the sun reflecting off the water shimmering that held carp cascading into the fountains. They finally got outside, blinded by the brightness Rose and Sebastian were driven to the hotel, she took his hand as he guided her to their room.

The hotel was magnificent and amongst the array of stunning artwork, they came to their room. Sebastian opened the door wide and in front of them was a sea view as far as the eye could see. The water shone like a million diamonds afloat above the ocean.

Rose gasped and ran to the window

"Sebastian you weren't joking were you, it's simply stunning!"

He shut the door and walked over, "I never joke." Sebastian walked off, "just going for a shower."

"Okay I shan't join you I'm tired so I might go for a lie down"

"No problem I'll poke you up in a bit"

Rose laughed.

"I adore your humour"

"I wasn't joking!" He said with a smirk on his face.

Rose's face blushed and she looked out to the ocean again and her eyes rested on the beach.

"Sebastian I'm going down to the beach," she shouted.

"Okay I'll see you down there in a bit"

Rose ran down the stairs, running her hand along the cool solid gold banisters, and peering out of every window. Touching the plush furniture she spun around, looking up to see the dizzying heights of the hotel and the amazing décor. She breathed in deep and took the moment in hand, running through the reception area and straight out onto the beach, she knelt down into the sand and sifted it through her fingertips.

"Ahhh sand, how I've longed for you to be between my toes," she said, taking off her shoes and pushing her feet into the sand.

Looking out to sea, the sun was setting, she walked out to the ocean where the sand was wet and dug her toes in sitting down on the wet sand.

Rose watched as the sun slowly set, there was a mild breeze gently blowing through her hair with the sand between her toes and her hands she leant back and watched as the ocean washed over the rocks and the sparkles reflected from the setting sun. She looked around her to see she was the only one on the beach. It was indeed for her a perfect moment. She felt like this was what her life had been leading to. Silently sat there her mind quiet, she fell into pure bliss, putting her head back to catch the last few rays of sun before it set, she felt the sand shift and looking to the side it was Sebastian.

"How are you feeling?"

"Peaceful" she said with a calm expression on her face enjoying the glow of the sun.

"Good"

"It's as if everything has fallen into place, nothing to worry about nothing to think about because this is all that matters here and now this moment"

"It takes you to travel to Cairo for you to feel peace within and be in the now?"

Rose frowned, "no not at all, it's sinking in, everything you have told me and it's coming into place bit by bit, but moments like these help it all fall into place."

"Amazing what the sun does to you when it sets, you should see it when it rises"

Rose looked over at Sebastian his eyes were as blue as the ocean in front of her and she was hypnotised.

"God was having a good day when he made you Sebastian"

He smiled and looked down at his feet under the wet sand, "God created many beautiful awe inspiring natures," he said, "you being one of them. And it may sound cliché but it's true Rose, you're simply amazing. The past you have put behind you, you have had a long and tiresome journey and you come out still shining, your light hasn't dimmed at all and I bask in your glow."

Rose cupped his chin. "Enough Sebastian I know I didn't believe your way of thinking the night we parted the first time I doubted all you said but here we are again!

Fate, coincidence, love, I do not know what brought us back together. We're here and now I want to learn from you, all that you know. I feel I'm ready and it's going to be long I know that, but I want to be where you are in body, mind and soul, I'm only partly feeling it at the moment, let me learn, please."

"Do you feel love Rose?"

She looked into Sebastian's eyes and said "with every inch of my body I feel you move through me. Your emotions, your gestures your admiration your everything I am you."

Sebastian looked down to the sand and shifted his finger through the grains. "I am going to briefly tell you how I work, and it's something of simplicity…you simply start by observing your emotions, note their presence, step back from it, get unstuck from that emotion. Notice the emotion and as soon as you do, the emotion fades. It's distracted because you're observing it and with that simple observation it stops."

Rose looked confused and shook her head for a moment

"But if you're observing your emotions endlessly, and they fade as quickly as you say they do, won't you become emotionless? You begin to feel nothing?"

Sebastian looked on into the distance, hearing what Rose had said he breathed deeply.

"No Rose you experience the emotion fully, as a wave coming and going, try not to block the emotion or push the emotion away, and don't try to keep the emotion around, just be witness to the emotion."

She looked at Sebastian with concern.

"So rather than acting upon emotion for example crying you just feel the emotion"

"Yes exactly that, you have to remember you are not your emotion, what you are thinking at that split second probably hasn't even happened in that split second. It's more likely a thought from the past or future which of course are illusions."

Rose looking confused as ever and turned to him quickly, "Sebastian, you're simply saying that rather than giving into the emotion you feel at hand you observe it and just leave it as it is? I understand it is an illusion but some parts of the past must be faced and tackled and dealt with and unfortunately with that comes feelings. You cannot by any means ignore your natural reaction to a past or future thought. The reaction you feel e g crying or anger is an emotion to that event, you're dangerously buckling your feelings down along with the reaction to that emotion, don't you think that's a tad risky?"

He looked down to his hands running his fingers over the lines of his palm.

"I don't see it as a risk, I see it as a coping mechanism, and this is me and this is how I am" he looked to Rose in slight anger.

Rose looked out to the sun setting and turned to him.

"Love has layers. It's never ending its eternity. It goes on as far as the eye can see, its hurt, it's laughter it's anger it feels and I don't know who we answer to at the end of it all, but knowing I have felt love I can say I can die happy."

Rose put her hand on his heart.

"Your heart is beating fast" she smiled

"It's how I am with you."

"Well I hope I don't give you a heart attack."

Sebastian laughed, "cheeky"

The sun began to set, and both were plummeted into darkness left with only the sound of the ocean. Rose fell into Sebastian's arms cold and shivering slightly in the cool evening breeze.

"Never let me go," she said weakly.

"I won't," he said kissing her forehead.

Rose could feel herself well up, she had never had anyone who had never let her go- everyone she knew had left her.

She had faith in Sebastian, yet felt slightly naive at that fact. She brushed the negative thought away, there was no need for it anymore, if she fell she knew Sebastian would be there to catch her and if he wasn't she would always pick herself back up again.

Rose turned to Sebastian

"Church wedding?" she laughed squeezing his arm.

"No not yet plus I don't think I believe in it all, the whole church and Christ and God after going through what I have been through. I believe we do have a God in all of us we give ourselves strength and courage, all we have to do is believe in ourselves. There's this wonderful old Italian joke about a poor man who goes to church every day and prays before the statue of a great saint, begging he says, *Dear Saint…*" Sebastian paused as Rose was laughing too much at his attempt of an Italian accent- "*please please….give me the grace to win the lottery.* This prayer goes on for months. Finally the exasperated statue comes to life, looks down at the begging man and says in weary disgust, *my son-please please buy a ticket.*"

Rose laughed. "Wait, the idea is that we humans are only SO strong. We get strength from our emotions. We are at our strongest emotionally when we have positive influences in our lives.

When we are loved, cherished, filled with joy, we are emotionally stronger than when we are alone, depressed, filled with sadness. For me Sebastian, God is infinite love, infinite acceptance. Faith, if done right is an unlimited supply of power. Allowing you to have the reserves to deal with life, faith is a form of mental energy-like love. It gives you the fuel we call bio-energetic resources to help deal with life. My basic social baseline theory is that-love and friendships are on an equal par with faith, when it comes to help us coping."

Sebastian looked to Rose in wonder shaking his head…

"Where did all that come from?"

She looked at Sebastian, his eyes intense as ever.

"My heart Sebastian, if you ever open it, and you ask the right questions the answers will come from the heart. Your heart will guide you to the knowledge you need to know"

She laughed nervously, "we have been talking about and thinking about and arguing about this for over two thousand years…we tend to be the experts on prayers."

"So many opinions are forced upon a generation that we care too much about what people think, religion etc. Can you imagine a world if Jesus hadn't been born? And what our world would be like?"

He raised his eyebrows in such a huge thought, looking at Rose exasperated

"It would be a horrible place. Truly awful."

Sebastian grunted- "Your bias is showing."

"Not really. Let's see- until Christianity, every concept of the worship of God was based upon the sacrifice of animals. All of them. From Jupiter to Mithras, to Kybele. You offered doves, bulls, cats and dogs. It was all bloodshed."

"Christianity does go on about blood an awful lot Rose," he quipped.

"But this time it is the God who gives his blood, not demands it. That was the change- never again would God demand blood sacrifice- now he gave it. And think about it- God was now on the side of the weak..."

"Hardly,"

"It's true. Here was a God whose followers focused on the poor, the weak, and the disenfranchised, the slave, the subjugated."

"All the better to start a revolt..."

"All the better to introduce compassion into this world."

Sebastian laughed, "Are you trying to suggest that Christians invented compassion?"

"Of course not," she playfully jabbed him, "But I will suggest they were the first religion to make it their main thrust."

Sebastian still grinning replied "I believe Buddhism pre-dates Christianity,"

"You know what I mean. You focus on the negative and never see the positive with Christianity."

186

"Call me a cynic," he sighs and gazes up at the stars.

"Imagine it Rose- a world without poverty, without division, food readily distributed across the world, a utopia…"

"This is what you think the world would be like without Christianity? Gee- I guess the Bronze Age pagans lived a life of utter bliss."

"No silly," he grins, "no religion full stop. No Gods at all."

"People need belief Sebastian," Rose said quietly, but he did not seem to hear.

"The ultimate revolution Rose; the ultimate triumph of the human spirit, the human intellect. The world without any religions. Oh, I don't think it will happen in our lifetimes, nor even our children's generation, but eventually. There is hope."

Rose smiled shaking her head. "So a reception wedding then!"

They both laughed, getting up they dusted each other down and walked back to the hotel.

Rose had a nap as Sebastian sorted the luggage out. He quietly placed a gift by her pillow.

A few hours later, yawning and stretching, her hand knocked a box off the pillow.

She opened it with excitement it was a ring. She slammed the box shut and held it to her chest.

No, she thought. *It can't be.*

She slowly opened the box again and took the ring out. It was solid platinum and inscribed inside the ring said "I love you for eternity." She felt her stomach leap, and put the ring on her finger, it fitted perfectly. Looking at her hand from afar it complimented her and she kissed the ring before looking up to see Sebastian in the doorway smiling.

"You like?"

Rose leapt off the bed and flung her arms around him.

"Are you sure you can trust me with your heart?"

"Rose if I had the world I'd trust you with it but seeing as I only have my heart to give I will give this to you"

"Wow"

Rose was astonished because she had never had anyone trust her so much.

"Don't doubt yourself Rose, ever! I can see that expression on your face when you screw your eyebrows you doubt your ability. I'm talking about creating your own reasons in life and making your way in the world. We're born into the world not knowing a thing no fear no hate, no anger but others implement those into us, and it's only us who decide if we take those emotions on board or not.

"We do not have to feel anger or sadness or fear, we control ourselves, opinions; you have to be strong enough to choose whether to take an opinion on board.

But again it's if you're strong enough and know yourself well enough to make or break an opinion of others. For example: There was a woman who was told she was no good in TV but she broke that opinion and became a multimillionaire and created her own TV show. Another was a man with dyslexia who was told he would never write a book there lies a man who is a self made millionaire who has wrote world renowned books.

We need to have the balls to break the old ways of life and believe in ourselves. We also cant be afraid to ask for help. So for example, you want to write a book but have no money, ask banks, friends, family. But in order to ask, you must believe in your own idea, confidence rubs off on people. You show that, and you will be on your way.

"If you show no confidence it instils a doubt in people's minds as to whether they should or help you out. Enthusiasm for the love of your idea goes hand in hand with confidence, but all of this starts and ends with you, no one else.

"You could have hundreds of friends tell you until they're blue in the face of how amazing a writer you are, how you're imaginative, that you'll be breaking boundaries of years of old aged rules and opinions giving way to fresh new thought provoking ideas.

However, if you do not believe those opinions you do not believe in yourself. If you doubt your every thought, your dream ends there and it lies before your feet. It is up to you to pick that dream up and run with it no matter the negative responses.

"No matter what you do in life there will always be a negative and a positive. There is one rule that will never die, you will never ever make everyone happy! So please don't ever doubt your power I trust you with my heart, all of it and that is a lot to ask from you. Do you trust yourself with my heart?"

Rose looked at Sebastian she stopped breathing and could feel herself falling into panic. However, she held her own, she thought, *I can't keep doing this whenever anyone challenges me I have to believe and trust myself.*

Her heart a flutter she breathed again. "Yes I do, I do"

Sebastian squeezed Rose tight and kissed her softly. "Thank you for being you."

He took Rose's hand and looked at the ring he kissed each finger tracing his kisses up her arm. She smiled knowing what it might lead to. Kissing her neck submerged her into bliss, his lips moulded to her earlobe sucking gently. Sebastian made sure to look into her soul as he gently placed his soft fingers on roses skin whispering.

"How does it feel?"

Demanding her attention, speaking was out of the question. Her lips pulsate in anticipation, Sebastian smiled, he knew this was what hunger looked like.

She was the ocean he was the earth, her hips moved with his rhythm, her soul was not her own and when she moan it was of ecstasy. He lit enough fire inside of her she could take down the earth. He gently absorbed himself into her engorged breasts. He took her nipples with his mouth and embraced her body, feeling the fleshy sculptured breasts under his hands.

Rose could feel him poised and throbbing. He merged himself against her body laying her down slowly into the settee, gently separating her legs. Rose surrendered, spiralling into a euphoric feeling. They kissed each other wiping the sweat from each other's face, both out of breath.

Smiling to one another, they lay there for a while until they fell back to reality; Rose looked out of the window from the bed.

"What time do you think it is! I'm getting pretty hungry!"

"Not sure hope it's not too late! Then again, we have room service! That could be lethal…"

Sebastian rolled off the bed and went to find the menu. As he walked he felt a strange sensation over his body. He went to the bathroom, locking the door and rested his head against the cool wood, whispering to himself.

"Why am I feeling this? I still haven't got answers….I don't want to see your face anymore."

He turned to the mirror and a whisper in his ear replied, "to find the answer look for the question"

Sebastian shook his head, clearing the voice away from him.

He looked into the mirror, and a visual thought shot through him from when he was younger. He sat in the arms of his mother as she strokes his hair. She whispers something in his ear and he drifts off to sleep in her arms as she rocks back and forth…then a sudden bang of a door and all goes dark. Sebastian peered back into the mirror, seeing tears gather in the corner of his eyes.

"NO… NO you caught me this once." He wipes the tears away harshly and walked from the bathroom.

Rose lay in bed looking up at the ceiling still naked and feeling euphoric.

Sebastian came back in with the menu "It all looks amazing and it's twenty four hours room service!"

Rose leapt up from the bed and looked through the menu.

"I want to try something different something I've never tried before"

Sebastian had a smile on his face; Rose looked up.

"What you smiling at?" Sebastian grabbed the menu from Rose.

"I'll choose the food and I'm going to do something for you!"

Rose looked perplexed..

"Okay fire away I'm ready."

Sebastian stepped out to make the call whilst she took a shower; he shouted, "all ordered on its way in about 30 minute."

Rose breathed in deep glad to be where she was. Listening to the crashing waves of the sea and looking directly out to the ocean as she showered, she felt serenity for the second time that day. Cairo was sinking into her soul, and loved the feeling.

The food arrived and Rose was in her dressing gown, Sebastian gestured for Rose to come sit on the settee

"I'm going to…." Before she could finish her sentence she felt something come over her eyes, he had blind folded her. A roaring grin sprinted across her face she loved this idea. Feeling giddy inside Rose shuffled back on the settee to get comfy, he leant over to start with the food

"This I will…"

He put the food to Rose's lips and gently traced it round.

"Don't lick, not yet"

She was eager to taste the sticky food it smelt amazing, Sebastian began to kiss Rose's lips.

"You taste sweet"

She could feel herself ablaze inside.

"You can taste"

She slowly traced her tongue along her silky lips.

"Ummm what was that? It tastes like sweet syrup?"

Sebastian put the dough against her lips.

"Bite"

She took a devouring bite from it and moaned in reckless pleasure.

"Oh my god Sebastian what was that?"

"Cheese cake, cream topping!" He laughed

After trying a further five more courses of falafel, hummus, and roasted lamb, Rose started to feel full.

"What was with the blind fold?" she asked as she took it off gently and smiled.

"When one of your senses is lost, others are heightened. Just to give you an example try eating the foods now without your blind you'll find your pallet is not so attentive. Rose took a bite from the food."

"Well I never! That is amazing I think I'll eat everything with my eyes shut from now on!"

"You would look a little odd Rose"

"Well you've just done yourself no favours Mr Lawrence showing me the next stage of tasting food it's brilliant!"

Sebastian laughed, "I'm aiming on having you try different things in your life so I'm glad you liked this one!"

"Well tick that off my list thank you,"

Sebastian looked up at the time. "Best I get to bed beautiful I have early lectures if you care to join me? I'm up at six in the morning though."

Rose looked in horror, "no thanks leave me in bed!"

A few weeks passed and they were both back in London.

Darkness fell around the room as Sebastian lay his head down. Before he knew it his alarm was blaring and, begrudgingly, moving his arm out of the warmth of the bed, he squinted from the bright light of his phone to turn the alarm off. Sebastian got up from his bed to walk to the bathroom holding his back and stretching.

"I'm getting to old to do these early mornings."

Standing in the shower letting the warmth of the water run over his neck and shoulders, he heard footsteps and Rose emerged into the bathroom. She opened the door slightly and popped her head in to find Sebastian smiling at her.

"Good morning, do you care to join me?"

She stepped into the shower and lay her head on his chest as the water cascaded over their bodies. Rose sighed, Sebastian took her head in his hands.

"Are you okay? What's with the sigh?"

Rose looked up to Sebastian and kissed him lightly. She ran her fingers over his lips and Sebastian moaned biting Rose's bottom lip slightly.

She nearly fell to the shower floor.

He shook his head sighed hard lent his head into the water and closed his eyes trying to steady his breathing.

"Fuck what is this?"

He felt a turn in his stomach, his body felt weak at the thought of her.

After teasing him in the shower Rose lay in bed as she watched Sebastian step out from the shower and dress in silence, he grabbed his satchel taking one look at Rose he smiled a little walked out, Rose frowned and buried her head back into the pillow.

Sebastian arrived at his lecture he began to feel a little surreal.

The colours around him became more vibrant almost blinding as if someone had just turned the colour up on everything around him. He stared at the trees out of the window and closed his eyes breathing deep.

He hoped the feeling and colours would die down as a headache was the last thing he needed. The students arrived in the room   looking over at Sebastian who was staring into thin air.

"Mr. Lawrence? Are you okay?" one of the students walked over to him clearing his throat. Sebastian looked up startled.

"I didn't hear you walk in sorry where were we?"

"Mr Lawrence you haven't started your lecture yet."

"Sorry my apologies I haven't been sleeping well"

"No problem so shall we begin professor?"

Sebastian looked out of the window and slowly he began walking out of the room.

Still in bed Rose heard a knock at the door. She got up sleepily and stumbling over her clothes she peeped through the door and saw it was Sebastian. She opened the door to him he was stood there in a defeated stance.

"Sebastian are you ok? I thought you were at a lecture today?"

"Not today" he said looking down.

"Sebastian you don't look right you seemed out of it this morning too have I done anything wrong?"

He walked through the door holding onto Rose as she guided him to the settee and sat him down.

"What's going on? Have I done something wrong please talk to me"

He looked up at her in a blank look. "You feel…" his voice trailed off.

"Sebastian you're scaring me what do you mean I feel?"

Still staring down he stood up and walked towards the bedroom where he stripped off and fell into bed.

"I must sleep please leave me be."

Rose looked on in a concerned manner

"Yes of course" she walked away closing the door tying her nightgown hesitantly whilst thinking.

Rose's phone rang she saw it was Sebastian's principle.

"Hello" she said in a worried tone

"Sorry to bother you Rose, but Sebastian has just walked out of a lecture is he with you?"

"Yes sorry he's asleep he's acting really unusual but I'll leave him to rest for now"

"Please keep an eye on him we are worried he's never done this before."

"Of course thank you for calling."

The phones clicked off and Rose looked behind her to see Sebastian standing behind her his eyes just wide open. He was not moving or blinking. Rose walked over slowly and waved her hand in front of his face.

"Sebastian go back to bed" she said sternly.

She gently grabbed his arm and as she did he put his hand on hers. Rose squinted her eyes unsure of what he was doing, she helped him back to bed where he put his head on the pillow and he closed his eyes.

Rose walked out of the room but left the door open. She pulled the settee to the bedroom and watched him sleep. She did not know why but she felt she had to keep an eye on him from afar; his behaviour seemed unusual giving Rose an unsettled feeling.

Three hours passed. Rose was drifting in and out of sleep but Sebastian wasn't sleeping. He was continually opening and closing his eyes in a slow motion, which gave concern to Rose. She walked over to him and stroked his face, there was no flinching or movement it was like he was in a trance and simply couldn't speak.

Rose whispered

"Sebastian? I'm going to do tea do you care for anything to eat?"

He said nothing so she got off the bed.Rose was thinking what would have caused this, was from this morning? She thought to call the hospital first but wanted to see if he would make any progress during the night.

As she was cooking, she could hear whispers from the bedroom. Rose walked over with curiosity and looked on as Sebastian was sat at the edge of the bed reading a book out loud to himself, she slowly walked over to him and sat next to him careful not to disturb him. She looked at the book it was just pure red, he was reciting a poem that was in it.

"To whom we owe this honour of our time here on earth and such elegance that graces our thoughts, the nature that is our everyday sound track to whom do we thank for this? The light that permeates my soul giving me all the happiness I need is overwhelming do I give thanks to thee, the very soul I hold within my crevice that is of my body and mind I give thanks to who created me from nothing. The bones that hold me to perceive this earth.

"Without the wonderful cascade that is of feeling the world around me, I look in awe of life around this being I hold so tight all that I view is that of the beholder of beauty and elegance, the bitterness too awe inspiring, relentless brutality that we create is a glorious velocity of feeling." Sebastian stopped and looked at Rose; he held her face in his hands and smiled at her, Rose smiled back nervously.

"Sebastian you're scaring me why are you reciting this?" she whispered

"Because I adore you" she looked over to the book he was reading but there was no words on the pages.

His eyes sparkled like never before, he blinked and he seemed to come out of a trance.

"Sorry Rose I'm still tired I'll sleep a little more I'll get back to work tomorrow." He recited in a monotone.

"If you're sure you're okay by then, I've done some food for you"

"I'm not hungry"

He turned away, put the book on the side table, and tucked himself into bed. Rose looked on and just shook her head before walking away to the kitchen. She sat at the bar of the table and pulled her plate of food to herself and started eating. Her thoughts were muddled and worried about Sebastian, unsure of what to do if he got worse.

Her thoughts went back to the people that know Sebastian. Seeming, as she doesn't know a lot about his past, so she rang Jen, his long standing stewardess. She went to find his brief case and took out his phone, she scrolled to Jen's number and hesitantly rang it. The phone rang and

Roses heart beat harder, afraid of what Jen might tell her and crossing her fingers that it wasn't going to be all bad: Jens voice interrupted Roses thoughts.

"Hello?" answering with urgency as Jen saw Sebastian's number flash up on her phone.

"Jen its Rose" she said sounding happy.

"Hi beautiful what can I do for you?"

You know Sebastian for longer than I have?"

"Yes, is everything okay Rose?" Concern laced her voice.

"Not really, he's acting strange Jen, he walked out of his lecture today and he's been on and off sleeping he's been reciting poems from plain paper and looking dazed."

Jen stood with the phone resting on her shoulder nearly dropping it. She looked over to her husband who was cooking and gave a sign of cut throat

"Okay look don't worry I think he has over worked himself, leave him to sleep I'll speak to him tomorrow look I've got to go we will speak soon sorry"

The phone clicked off and Rose stood there in disbelieve. Why had Jen been so cold and off with her? Something wasn't adding up.

Jen put the phone down and shot a look of shock to James.

"What's up Jen?"

"James I think, I think he's starting to defend," she said spritely

"Really?" James replied in disbelief.

"Yes I think Rose has something…"

"What do you think it could be? I mean, you know should we keep an eye on him for her?"

"No, let it be James… Remember what happened last time" Jen looked down in concern.

"Yes" he nodded and closes his eyes.

The Friday dawned it was a sunny day and Rose woke up on the couch with a crick in her neck from sleeping awkwardly. She got up slowly to see that Sebastian had gone from his bed, Rose shot up, ran to the bedroom and noticed a note on the side cabinet telling her he had gone to work.

Rose stood there bit her lip and looked worried. She hoped he was feeling much better but somehow didn't believe it. She walked to the kitchen to clean the house and distract herself.

When Sebastian arrived at the university the principle came over.

"Sebastian good to have you back I heard you weren't too well yesterday"

"I'm fine sir, back to my normal self."

"Good to hear"

Sebastian lowered his head in defeat and walked into the lecture hall, standing there among the array of chairs he sighed. The students started to make their way into the lecture hall, Sebastian stood there in the mood to talk about religion and give his straight opinions. And so, the lecture started.

RELIGION

"Many say Religion has been around ever since an ape began considering death. I am not of this belief. Religion is not simply an idea or consideration of what may happen when a person dies. Is that not simple philosophy? A true religion has rules and regulations. It has ideals, a moral code, "true" stories about people who have followed a code and the punishments for those who did not. Thousands used to inspire creativity that would be impossible without it, believe a religion. Used to justify acts of evil that others would call murder in the form of Martyrdom and sacrifice. I grew up in a strongly Catholic household and one of my first memories is passages being read from the bible to me by my mother. I remember one story in particular. The story of Job.

"This story started with a man who had everything he could ever want, a family, money, a household and of course God's love. Then God was convinced by Satan to allow him to test the man, providing he was not killed. Satan then put Job through the most horrible of times in order to test his Faith and try to make him hate god. He killed the man's family, likely strong believers in God themselves. He killed all the man's animals and burned His house to the ground. He made Job a beggar and attacked him with sores and pain. Yet the man held Faith in god. All I can ask here is why? If this is the famous love of God then I hope someone kills God soon. He allowed his son to be tortured and slaughtered and for what? Our sins? I doubt it. Frankly I don't think god could look down on us and protect us. Looking through most of the New Testament it seems every religious leader is executed in some horrific manner or another. Yet humanity looks no less sinful to me.

"In fact, let us look at Satan for a moment. The famous fallen angel Lucifer who was proud of his position and so he was cast down. He then does everything he can to fight back against god. Yet when god's enemies die, he tortures them in hell? Bullshit! If Satan existed then he would reward these people for standing against god like he did himself. And even pride itself. Name one person you know who isn't proud of themselves when they accomplish something. I know someone who is proud of the fact that they are humble. This religion forbids us from following our nature. It says lust is a sin. Yet it is lust that brought that same preacher into existence. Why would a God who designed us make us go against the very instincts he gave us?

" I went travelling to America a few years ago and I saw protests against abortion. There was a girl walking in who was no older than thirteen. She had been raped a few weeks ago and she was sobbing. Her parents had disowned her and she had no support at all. Yet the crowd screamed at her, called her foul things and threw things at her. I phoned the police with video evidence of this and the crowd were arrested but were shrieking all the while about sin. Sebastian shuddered at the memory.

"This is what religion does to people. Religion is not a belief, but a control method usually leading to violence. Terrorists today call out their religion from the rooftops and blow themselves up in its name. Religion has caused crusades, massacres, genocides and bullying. The world would be better without it."

The students sat there stunned.

"Any questions at all anyone?"

They were just sat looking at each other in shock.

"Strong opinions I know but I know there will be a lot of people out there willing to fight for their opinion, I know of this, but the fact being that you can argue until you're blue in the face. The world of opinions will never change to just one correct answer."

A hand slowly raised to ask a question

"Yes in the back"

Sebastian stepped forward to look at her.

"I don't even know where to begin. There is so much you said there that deserves argument."

"Go ahead. I never shy from one." Sebastian said smiling.

"Firstly, your definition of a religion. Yes, religions have rules and regulations. But not all are used to justify acts of cruelty."

"But they could be. Name me a religion that has not had its doctrines or even its belief used to justify such things?"

The woman paused and said, "Taoism."

"Good choice. But not true."

"Jainism"

"I will accept that, but must point out all that leads to, is confirming my statements about religion are true, with the possible exception of Jainist belief. Possibly."

"Fine. Then your statements on Satan."

"What about them?"

"You are rather biased towards Milton's portrayal of the Devil are you not?"

Sebastian smiled, "Paradise Lost I find a bit long winded."

"What about our Muslim interpretation of Satan?"

"What about it?"

"Under that one Satan isn't all evil per se; rather he does what he does because Allah orders him to do so. To Muslims, ALL things are obedient to the will of Allah That includes Satan. He torments mankind not because of pride or arrogance, but because Allah wills it so."

"Which suggests God sends evil into this world yes? Please- I thought you were disagreeing with me, not reinforcing my arguments?"

"Fine. Consider then the argument as to why he fell. According to the Sufi's, God creates man, and they are the most perfect creation. He orders his angels to bow down to them but Satan will not. According to the theory he loves God so he will not bow to any except him. Even if God tells him to. So he is expelled from the presence of God. And Satan does not blame God- he blames man. He sees this creation- mankind itself beloved of God and feels they are unworthy. So he goes out to prove to God, whom he loves beyond all things, that his creation is unfit for such adoration. He does not punish mankind because he is evil; he tempts and punishes mankind because he thinks we are weak and unworthy of the love of the Creator."

"Go on," said Sebastian quietly.

"Consider then THAT version of your Satan figure. He would punish all those who rebelled against God. He would be the ultimate agent provocateur; endlessly seeking to incite humans to rebel against Gods rules and then happily punishing them. There is no contradiction and there is no paradox. Indeed think about it- under that definition then Satan is the most devout, the most fanatical worshipper of God. He exists as arguably the ultimate standard bearer in the worship of God- one unwilling to bend the knee at all, even when commanded to by God himself. Correct?"

Sebastian said nothing, his eyes fixed upon the woman speaking to him.

"And regarding your comment about religious fanatics, You realise that when speaking of the current incarnation of say Muslim terrorism, you refer to less than half of one percent of the total Muslim population on Earth yes? Yes, religion has caused wars, and crusades and conquest and all those things. But it doesn't hold exclusivity. The greatest war in human history never had anything to do with religion except the deliberate murder of millions of a single faith by one side. Stalin and Mao never had religion to justify their massacres of tens of millions of peoples. Religions don't have exclusivity upon being an utter bastard you know."

The girl swallowed and pressed on. "I am not saying religion cannot be abused of course it can- so can anything. Your words earlier- there is nothing to stop someone in this room from hearing them, agreeing, and going out and committing a crime against humanityclaiming your words motivated them. You would of course condemn such a thing, but you can't stop it. Humans will leap upon anything they can to justify their own actions. And what is your ultimate aim? To ban religion? To forbid the millions of people who happily get on with life and find hope and love in their faiths, just because you think religions are a bad thing. That would cause chaos."

Sebastian nodded and held up a hand.

"You are correct. And this is why I should probably never be allowed to be the ruler of the world." Laughter began around the lecture hall, and he smiled, "or even a politician."

The young lady smiled and she looked at him. "Your views are interesting, but you must admit- they are based upon Christian theology yes? You were raised in this nation; raised in a Christian household yes?"

Sebastian nodded.

"Have you considered that we Muslims have our own world views? I do not think so. And as much as you seem to know about other religions, you don't embrace what they show."

"Which is?"

"The sheer diversity in the way we worship God. Nothing else so marks humans as unique as the way they decide the worship God. Indeed when you take it like that- then it redefines your views."

"How so?"

"Yours is just another voice in the great tumult of voices. Yours is just another soul trying to make sense of the world, just like the rest of us, and you define your struggle by the models you grew up with. You grew up Christian; you see the world in Christian terms. I grew up Muslim; I see it likewise in my way."

"Are you saying I cannot transcend my own culture?"

"If you cannot see what holds you back Professor, how on Earth can you transcend it?"

Sebastian was done. "Okay guys good argument, please keep reading your books and studying and I will test you further next week, class dismissed." He sat down at his desk, watching as the students filed out, he was tired. As the last person left he followed after them shutting the lights off behind him.

THE ARGUMENT

He put his briefcase on the floor of the apartment with his heart beating hard, he walked over slowly he sat down next to Rose. She held his hands in hers and looked directly into his eyes.

"You had me worried yesterday, you were out of sorts, you're not working too hard you seemed fine a few days ago, is there something you're not telling me?"

"I'm not having an affair if that's what you think Rose," he laughed

"No I know, but your past, it's jaded….you never speak of it and when I confront you, you deflect the question, because of what happened yesterday I'm thinking your now is conflicted with this unspoken truth."

" Rose there is a reason for everything in my life and the way I am"

"You were reading a poem last night about emotions you read it with such heart like you were wanting something but pulling back from what comes naturally to others"

"What comes naturally Rose?"

She bowed her head, "I'm unsure of what you're capable of Sebastian, you're becoming unpredictable a side I've never seen. How can I trust a man who denies his past, and in a cloud of what made you who you are today?"

"All that matters is I'm here now, my past is my past. Rose please I beg don't push this…"

"Why not? Why can't I push to know you Sebastian it's been years now, it's like you're a shadow."

"A shadow that has protected me over the years Rose, please don't do this now"

"You also never dream."

Sebastian shot a look to her, "how do you know this?"

"I can tell you remain so still there is no REM from you at all you don't jolt in bed or make no noises you hardly sleep"

"Don't over think."

"I'm not I'm knowing what I see, what I witness is fact!" Rose started to breakdown and cry, her frustration gaining momentum.

"Please I beg don't do this, my past is not ordinary I sincerely can't remember it and I don't know what it will take to break me from it."

Rose took Sebastian's chin in her hands and looked at him. "Me, it'll take me."

He pulled his head away from hands.

"Rose I'm warning you don't push me to something I don't know of."

Getting angry Rose stood up over Sebastian, "how could you not know your past Sebastian it's breaking you down slowly. I don't want to lose you why are you doing this to me?"

"It's not you I'm doing this to"

"It feels like it"

"It's not and it's not my problem you feel that way, I don't care for how you feel Rose I protect me to protect you"

Rose stood back slowly tears streaming from her eyes and her face flushed with anger shaking her head she asked, "did you really just say that to me?"

"Rose shit I'm sorry" he reached out to her but she hit his hand away.

"No I can't do this"

"Rose please for God's sake I'm sorry is that not enough for you? Why can't you just be simple and take my apology first hand?"

"What are you saying to me right now Sebastian? This isn't you"

"This is me all of me, there is nothing else to me but this"

"I can't accept you for who you are now or ever, it's like you're created from nothing. No past, no life, no feelings"

Sebastian stood there staring at Rose, a blank expression crossed his face and he walked out the door.

"Where are you going?"

The door slammed shut and she sat defeated on the settee. She looked into space and just put her head into her hands.

Sebastian called Ralf to collect him outside

"Where do you care to go sir?"

"Just drive me anywhere Ralf I need to just…."

"Yes sir"

PREQUEL THERAPY.

With a faint sound of a ticking clock in the background, Sebastian sits calmly as the therapist. Daniel taps a pen against his lips. He sits forward.

"So…Sebastian what's happening? Any breakthrough?"

Sebastian straightens his tie, shifts in his chair, and crosses his feet.

"I'm in love that's a start?"

Daniel sits up in his chair, "um okay good, when and who and how long for?"

Sebastian sits up and brushes his shoes off nervously.

"I met her a few weeks ago she's a student but not of mine, she just turns up to my lectures, her name is Rose she's…" he looks down and frowns…his voice trails off and he clears his throat, pushing his glasses up his nose.

Daniel shifts his weight in his chair looking concerned he leans forward tilting his head to the side.

"Sebastian it's only been a few weeks"

"I know, it's not lust it's deeper…I think?, I felt something stir within me, something awakened that I've never felt before"

"Go on" Daniel replied intrigued.

"There's something about Rose, her innocence, she seems lost but comfortable with it, and I can be myself with her you know the type I mean?"

Daniel flicking through his notes "ah yes, action speaks louder than words and looks can say a thousand words" he reads from Sebastian's personal notes.

"Yes this is how I see"

Daniel shifts in his seat, "so you don't sense anything other than her look of love?"

"I see instead" he sharply replies.

Daniel looks down defeated, "so what you're saying is that you see love in Rose's eyes but you don't sense love within yourself?"

"Just the looks we give each other, like we understand each other"

"But Seb you said you don't believe in love at first sight?"

"Well that's because I've never seen it and now I have"

"You're supposed to feel" Daniel snapped, he sits back in his chair with an air of judgement.

"This will be an experience for you both," he states in a tired tone.

"Indeed it will if I ever see her again"

"What do you mean?" confused.

"Well she got too close. I had to go back to London, we are both in very delicate stages in our lives and I said that time heals and fate if I'm correct will guide us back together"

"But Seb" Daniel stands up abruptly. "You've waited ten years for something like this to come along and you leave it to fate?" He clicks his pen impatiently pacing the length of the room.

"I had a hunch, too many emotions are raw at the moment I have guidance and knowledge and Rose has none, but I know she walks the same path as I do when it comes to seeing. "

Daniel gritted his teeth. "Feeling" he says in a harsh tone.

"Ok what if…" Daniel says in a playful tone.

"What if what? My fate fails me, I never see her again, I lose the love of my life, my answer to my question? Happiness for eternity? I'm not thinking of that, it's in the future you know I live in the now." He snaps back.

Daniel rubs his forehead and Sebastian looks up to Daniel who is pacing back and forth. "Look" Seb sits forward in his chair.

"I know she has my answers but I feel I am not ready for her, am I really ready to face something that I have been wanting to know all my life? Am I ready to bring forth all that I have held back all these years? Will I lose my sense of self? There is so much at stake!"

"Jesus Seb, it's been years, do you want to sit in the dark wondering what if? Don't you want to see the light at the end of the tunnel now?" Daniel sits down in defeat "Well I only hope for your sake that fate is on your side, it's a delicate hand you're playing"

"I know, I believe if you want something so bad it will come again and I'm sure if its right I will be ready next time around, actions speak louder than words"

Sebastian's thoughts fade back to the present.

Rose stood and walked to the bedroom. She sat on her bed defeated and took her diary from her bedside cabinet.

GIVEN

When you're young there are no ideas for the future only the moment at hand exists- fun, carefree, but at what point does the balance subside to adulthood? When does the fun turns to responsibility, carefree turn to worries and the future creeps in like an unwelcome visitor.

Friends come and go leaving a trademark of their past on you, making you a little wiser to the world ahead.

Relationships free flow, and love stunts all that may grow. Our hearts flourish to then be broken with a slow healing in sight. Families are always there if not in front but always in the background, what you feel for them will subside (anger, hate) when they leave your side.

From when you're born to the day you die….what had you given in your life? To those who have touched your soul, your thoughts your laughter your being. There are 7.5 billion bodies that walk this earth emotionally connecting through laughter, stories, sadness, the list is endless. You matter in life among the billions, your words, your past affects those around you. As each day passes, we die a little more, so to give yourself to friends and family, lovers, it is not so bad, because each day we say goodbye we never know if it is our last.

"Sir I've been driving for four hours are you sure you want me to keep going?"

"That's fine Ralf just drop me off at home it's okay"

"Yes sir"

Rose sat crying at her diary, the door opened and Sebastian stood at the bedroom door. He walked over and knelt by her side.

"I apologise. It was not my intention to hurt you Rose please forgive me and my rudeness"

Wiping her tears away she asked, "you were callous and cold, how could you not care how I feel?"

"Rose I don't know where to begin, this is a journey I have to deal with myself.

it will take time so bear with me it's not like a written book you read of someone's past and they can't move on from it the usual template that every book goes by, I'm a complicated case Rose, and I can't, " he stopped himself and stood up to walk away.

"I'll sleep here tonight if you don't mind?"

"But I want you with me, we're so disconnected at the moment"

"I need space to breathe I'm going through something that has changed me slightly."

"Well I hope it's for the better"

"As do I"

He walked into the cupboard and grabbed some pillows and bedding, he took one last look at Rose who sat on their bed with her head hung and her eyes closed.

Sebastian tucked himself in to the settee hoping sleep would consume his thoughts; he grabbed his diary from the bottom of the settee and began writing.

FALLEN

I heard a saying once, that we fall so we can pick ourselves up. This never made any sense to me. I've fallen so many times in my life it's not the falling that is the hard part anymore, it's the picking yourself back up and gaining back the trust and the faith, you lost whilst falling.

The worst part is when you hit the ground and you shatter. You wonder where you have gone, if you will be the same and you cannot find that answer until you regain strength to stand life again.

My experience is that after falling you learn and it becomes ingrained in your senses of how not to fall so hard next time, because each time you step into a friendship or relationship you will fall, but it's you who decided how hard you hit the ground and how long your down for.

After my last fall, I shattered and I didn't want to be picked up I wanted to be left with my splintered soul, broken bones, and the hate that consumed me whole.

Not everyone wants to be picked up or even try for themselves, leave me to wallow in my own self-pity a while longer, I wish at times I could plug my feelings into someone and have them hurt the way I did/do/have. Then they would step back and walk away.

I managed to pick myself up slowly after a year but I am expecting to fall again but I know instead of hitting the ground I will break myself within an inch of my life.

The morning came with a bright gleam from the sun that peeked through the curtains. Rose got up from her bed rubbed her eyes and walked to the living room to find Sebastian just stood at the window looking out over the city.

"Sebastian, did you sleep well?"

He did not turn to face her or answer her question.

"Sebastian are you alright?"

He still looked out over the city with no flinching.

Rose walked over to him and waved her hand in front of his face he does not move.

"Sebastian please talk to me you're scaring me."

Rose stepped back and touched his hand; Sebastian moved his head and smiled at Rose.

"Good morning beautiful, I've just woke up I slept well"

Rose looking in disbelief, "Sebastian how long have you been standing there for?"

"Where?"

"The window Sebastian the window you're staring at the window and you weren't responding what is wrong with you?"

"I don't understand Rose I've just woke up and you're there saying morning to me? Why are you crying?"

"Jesus Sebastian you've been acting weird all week long, you're not sleeping you're staring out of windows with no movements or flinching you don't even blink!"

"Sorry I don't mean to scare you. Something is happening & I'm not sure what it is but I'm sure I'll be fine, it feels like a veil but I'm sure it'll pass probably because I've not been sleeping well?"

"A veil? From what?

"I don't know Rose but I'll be fine, I'm getting dressed for work now"

Sebastian walked off to the bedroom and Rose shook her head as if it was all a bad dream.

As Sebastian was getting dressed Rose sits back on the sofa she puts her head back. Her eyes closed and she drifted off....

Dream1

She dreams she is asleep. She watches herself wake up and she finds herself in bed then she wakes up and finds herself in bed again. It goes on until she awakes and finds herself in bed next to Sebastian. She gets up and she is shaking and sweating.... She turns to Sebastian and tries to wake him up. She shakes his arm and he wakes up from a heavy sleep

> *"What's up?"*

> *"Have I skipped a day? I thought you were going to work a minute ago but its dark outside.*

> *"Rose I've already been to work, It's Tuesday now," he sleepily snaps back.*

Rose sits there in utter disbelief.

> *"What happened to Monday?"*

> *"Rose get some sleep please we have a busy day tomorrow."*

> *"Okay" she shakes her head and frowns.*

Rose turns herself back into bed and shuts her eyes hoping she is still dreaming.

THE FALLEN

The day dawned it was now a Tuesday. Rose woke up to find Sebastian not in bed, but could heard footsteps on the floor of the house. Rubbing her eyes hard she sat still listening to the footsteps above her head. She jumped out of bed, worried and scared and ran to the balcony, to see Sebastian sitting on the roof with his legs hanging down. Rose's heart beat faster jumping into her mouth.

"What the fuck are you doing up on the roof Sebastian? Get down now or you'll fall!"

"Maybe it's the falling that will wake me up Rose, I've always been too afraid to fall if I let go will it really hurt?"

"What the hell are you on about Sebastian?"

"I don't know what's happening Rose, it's all new and it's scaring me"

"Please Sebastian get down and we can talk about this let me help you"

"Of course I don't even know how I got up here, don't cry Rose I'll find the fire escape somewhere."

"For fucks sake Sebastian just get in here you're giving me a heart attack!"

Sebastian slowly walked off from the roof and down the fire escape. As he stumbled into the living room, a very angry Rose stood shaking with anger.

"This will be the last stunt you pull now because it's getting tiring, what do you mean you're scared of falling?"

"I don't know Rose my thoughts speak for me now it's like I've been taken over..."

"Are you hiding something Sebastian? Is your subconscious trying to tell you something?"

"I want to know what happened in my past Rose, I think something has blocked it for so long now I don't know which way is up anymore."

Rose winced a painful relief but was still unsure of what Sebastian was yet to go through to reveal his past.

"Okay, well I don't want to discuss this anymore, you have a lecture and I'm due in with you so get changed and I'll meet you there."

"Yes yes of course I have a lecture today," he says nodding quickly.

Rose looked on with concern as he walked away.

FALLEN GLORY

Sebastian stood silently in the lecture hall. He peered amongst the array of chairs; empty, quiet and dark! He sighed deeply and wondered aloud, "where am I going?"

The students started to fill the room and so Sebastian began:

"Thank you for coming to the May lecture today, I'll be starting with Fallen Glory.

"The idea of Fallen Glory refers to the paradoxical figure of Satan in human literature. I assume you have done the pre-reading required for today's lecture, so I will not go into great detail about every nuance of how this figure has been viewed over the last few thousand years. I will point out however, that this supposed enemy of God generates much debate, much thought, much argument by Theists; so much you have to wonder why, inevitably, people always give him the best one-liners? Why at the end of the day he is presented as ultimately- cunning beyond compare, brilliant and rarely defeated except by some homespun wisdom.

"It actually makes you ask a simple question- given that Satan is seen as incredibly intelligent, wise beyond years, cunningly personified, utterly brilliant in his evil schemes- why on earth would such a creature turn against God in the first place?

And why on earth would such a creature then punish Gods enemies? Surely these are the people he most needs? His natural followers?

"When we get into the depths of Christian dogma we begin to see however that it is not just the Devil who has seemingly paradoxical behaviours. God does this. Indeed we can argue that there are grounds for Gods schizophrenic behaviour. After all, as was codified back in the 11th century, God is personified by three separate 'parts'. Would it be wrong to describe them as 'personalities'? The Father is, the Creator the Son is, the Sacrifice; and the Holy Spirit is, the Grace. Maybe I am showing my bias here, but surely the idea of one in three is a nice theological way of covering up that maybe there are three separate deities here and nobody wants to admit it? Or maybe the schizophrenic nature of God is genuine. After all, look at the basis of the Satan stories- there is this God, imbibed with multiple personalities and along comes Lucifer, who is arrogant, but this arrogance is arguably merely an extension of his creators; however his creator then says 'you are too arrogant, I will cast you out of heaven'. Does any of this make sense?"

The students laughed and the door opened. Rose walked in and his eyes were drawn to her, "Thank you for joining us Rose; we were just about to examine the supposed schizophrenia of God."

"I demand a second opinion on that diagnosis," she said taking a seat, eliciting more laughter and Sebastian smiles and carries on.

"Indeed. And I should be able to provide evidence to my own diagnoses yes? So then, let us look to the ways God demands worship shall we? We are told God is all loving, all caring, all forgiving yes? And this is true, to a degree. But he is not any of those things to worshippers of other Gods. He is after all, openly jealous of them."

A tall student, neatly dressed didn't put his hand up but rather stood up from his seat. "I think you are being rather selective in your interpretation of Old Testament teachings Professor."

"Probably," smiled Sebastian, "But let us just look at one small section of Old Testament teachings shall we?"

The student, all eyes upon him, shifted uncomfortably and nodded.

"Deuteronomy chapter twelve, verses two and three- does that not tell us to go out, find the sacred places of other Gods and destroy them, be they on hills, under trees, on mountains. It specifically says smash their alters; to obliterate the names of the Gods from that place. Does this not suggest he was being anything but loving?"

"But Professor- if you read on in Chapter twelve, you will find from that point basically all the way to the start of chapter fourteen, its all predicated upon preventing corruption of this Jewish faith by the faiths of the lands they are moving into. Indeed given the harshness of the measures, given it goes to say suggest that people are worshipping these foreign Gods, or are being tempted to by family members, that perhaps they are merely the measures taken to protect the faith?"

"Yes," Sebastien replied, "as it states that if your brother, or your mother, or your son, or your daughter, or your spouse or even your best friend says 'Let us go worship other Gods';- then you must kill them. It does not mince words."

"As I said sir, it could be protective measures." Murmurs arose around the lecture hall.

"Killing your family is the least harsh method; if its someone from another town who worships another God, not only do you kill them, but you burn the town and hand out their belongings- which I am sure would be open to abuse."

"With respect- that punishment is supposedly only reserved for the 'sons of Belial' yes?"

Sebastian held up a hand.

"Wait young man; I think it's only fair on others we step back a moment. It is clear both you and I have poured over the Book of Deuteronomy, but most here have not. And I have this feeling; we are going to spend hours doing this, agreed?"

"I could happily argue all night professor."

"As could I," Sebastian smiled, "I will arrange a time and place and before any, you and I can happily conduct a war over the meaning of the rules of that book if you want?"

The student smiled and asked, "mind if I bring a rabbi?"

"Of course. I look forward to being humiliated," he quipped, eliciting more laughter from the students as the one who was stood sat down.

He looked out across the room and nodded.

"Thus we see the folly and also the endless entertainment of dogmatic debate- but for me this illustrates a more general point I wish to make, which concerns reactions to these laws. The rules which the Bible give its followers in the worship of God, have led to others finding more simple, arguably more balanced ways of worshipping God. Take for example Le Vay's Satanic Bible."

His words gained a few raised eyebrows and he smiled- "I don't like the title much; indeed I wonder how much Le Vay chose the name just to shock Christians into a moral outrage, but be that as it may, this book contains a more balanced way of worshipping God. For myself I like to see it as an inheritor of more balanced pagan beliefs existent before Christ was born."

A tall dark skinned student raised his hand with alacrity and Sebastian nodded- "Mr Origari?"

"Tell me professor; do your 'balanced' pagan beliefs include the sanctioned prostitution of the Babylonian cities? Or the sacrifice of human babies in the worship of Baal in Carthage?

Simply- no. I will concede that getting into specific line by line arguments of Biblical dogma is folly, and bogs one down on specifics, so let us proceed to the general gist of pagan beliefs, the same broad sweep?"

The student seemed unhappy but nodded in agreement.

"So, let us make general points about the mainstream Bible and general sweeping points about pagan beliefs as found in the Satanic one, and go from there? Yes? Right. So, in a general sense, the bible states that ego, greed, pride, envy, sloth and lust are all frowned upon. They are classified as the seven deadly sins. The Satanic Bible does quite the opposite- it shows how these seven states are not sins but rather things that define us. I will ignore the fact that Le Vay got to write the so called Satanic Bible with thousands of years of hindsight; the seven deadly sins as they are called, exist because people do not know the limits of them...."

"No," Rose said stubbornly.

"Certainly sounds like it Rose," Sebastian pressed.

"Let me put it this way Professor. Rules exist because people did bad things and someone went 'hey- let's not allow that bad thing happen again." I remember laughing once about there being a rule in the Bible which says it is a sin for people to see a blind person walking past and tripping him up so you can laugh at him."

The room grinned and a few stifled their laugher.

"Think about it professor- that rule exists because once, as the tribes of Israel wandered the deserts seeking the promised land, someone was bored, saw a blind guy walk past and decided it would be bloody funny to trip him up and watch him fall. So a rule was made."

"Your point?"

"Rules come about because someone, usually an arsehole, does something that upsets everyone else. Tripping up a blind person is horrible. Normal people would be outraged. Not for religious reasons, but because they have empathy. They would make rules banning that. That's not religion- that's just basic common sense."

"So rules like this are merely manifestations of a decent empathic society?"

"Yes."

"And they will be expressed via the methods available to a society in order to prevent people breaking said rules again?"

"Yes."

"And while today we have police and parliament, back then they would utilise say religion?"

"Yes."

"Thank you Rose- you have just finalised my point that at their heart religions are used as control methods for those who cannot control their senses or urges. Hence why I feel that religion will never die out, because there are perhaps too many people who will never know their limits."

"Perhaps Professor, Rose says, It's because we want rules, that we need the rules. Perhaps all through human history we have tried to live in societies without these rules. And each time learned that the grass is not greener without said rules." Rose paused with baited breath but Sebastian merely smiled.

"Perhaps, but that's it for today. I will see you all next week."

Chatting and talking amongst themselves the students filed out; a few remained to ask Sebastian questions, which he answered, and even arranged a date for his inevitable ambush by the Bible quoting student and probably a Rabbi. Until, at last, he was alone with Rose. Rose sighed.

"What you see as a weakness, I see as a strength."

"What do you mean?"

"Sebastian, you point out the contradictions and the differing mentalities found in the Bible. You say this like you are the first person to know this. Christians have known this for thousands of years. They have debated it, argued over it, and defined themselves by these differences."

"And you have endless conflict between the Christian faiths…"

"Agreed. But you also have something else. Something you fail to take on board."

"And what's that?"

"Survival. The main reason the Christian faith has been so successful is because it is a broad thing. Because people can find the parts they like and focus on them. It allows itself be reinvented again and again."

"And each time you just add to the confusion," Sebastian said vaguely.

"Maybe. But I ask you- can you name me something else that has lasted for two thousand plus years? Bottom line, all crap aside, you cannot refute the simple fact that this messy, contradictory and sometimes bewildering faith has succeeded far more than any other. Two billion followers in every nation on Earth. It has outlasted every Empire, every nation, and every despot. It has lasted longer than damn near everything, with the exception of a handful of other religions. And that's really the test for your pagan beliefs isn't it?"

"What is?"

"You venerate this single approach, this single way of doing things. And maybe you are correct Sebastian. But I tell you what- let's give it a thousand years shall we? Too harsh? Okay, how about two hundred years. Just two hundred years. One tenth of the time the Christian faith has existed. Then tell me it's working."

"I hardly think that's fair."

"Don't you? I will bet you if that satanic bible still exists two hundred years from now, it will have bits added. Or commentary added. An extra book maybe. Why? Because that's us. That's humans. We are messy and we make rules and the rules are great and then something comes up- things we never imagined, and we try and cope. And usually we make new rules to cope with the new things. Or maybe we disagree over a rule and someone ignores it and someone else doesn't. Now you have schism. And so on. And that's faith Sebastian. That's humans. There is no single set of rules that has lasted any length of time. Ever."

"The pagan beliefs have survived far longer than Christianity."

"No they haven't. The Satanic bible was written in the sixties. Wiccan faith was invented in the 1920's. Right now you have people in Nordic country reinventing worship of Thor and Odin again. Sure these are based on older things- but they are not the older ways. Look at the version you give- its rather rooted in twentieth century values is it not? Seeking consent, based upon respect for the individual. Same as all the new age beliefs who claim to be ancient. But the ancient beliefs practiced sacrifice of humans. They killed prisoners and they sacrificed. The societies they emerged from and helped shape were barbaric. The steppe nomads never brought enlightenment, the Vikings made war upon the world and the Romans didn't need religion to go butcher everyone. They just did it because they could."

She sighs, "The world changes, but humans don't Sebastian. We cannot. We use religion because it's easily manipulated, but in the end, we will do horrible things because we can do horrible things. We take simple things and we complicate them. We always do. It's in our nature. We cannot change who we are."

Sebastian had gone very quiet. Rose saw his eyes glaze and felt him being lost into the depths of his own brain. She rubbed his hand and smiled.

"Look, in the end your belief is YOUR belief. If it helps you, helps you in anyway, then I love it. It's good. Go with it."

"Good, let's go home I'm starved," he said grabbing Rose's hand and kissing it softly.

Ralf meanwhile stood outside waiting by the car.

"Hello, where is it to be?"

Sebastian stood by the car tapping his finger on his lips thinking Rose looked up to him.

"Fingerless."

Rose burst into laughter, "what in God's name?"

"Just wait for it"

They both hopped in and Ralf drove them.

"So Rose you ever heard of the ontological argument?"

"We're not in lecture now you know!"

"I know but I like talking about it"

"Go ahead, the argument"

"The ontological argument says, you can define God into existence. If God is perfect, then existence being perfection, means you must exist, the aim is to find existence if you don't exist you can't be perfect if you do exist you can be perfect..." Sebastian faded in his voice and looked out of the window.

Rose looked at him with concern and asked "hey are you okay?"
Sebastian still staring out of the window shook his head.

"Sebastian you didn't make sense then explain"

"I can't it doesn't matter"

Rose laid her head on his shoulder and the car pulled up outside the restaurant.

"We're here"

"Thank you Ralf we shouldn't be too long I'm tired and I have a long day tomorrow."

They both stepped out and Sebastian grabbed Rose's hand and guided her into a dark room with very little light, a beautiful woman half dressed with fabric draping her tiny frame of a body seated them.

"Good evening, my name is 'I am' and I will be your hand servant for tonight, have you been before?"

Rose looked astonished.

"Hand servant?"

"Here we feed you by our hands, you can't use your own and there are no knives or forks. We hand feed you everything, but don't worry we're very hygienic it's another experience."

"Oh wow ummm okay let's do this!"

Sebastian smiled, asked for drinks, and swayed off to the music. The room was draped in soft fine fabrics a light delicate fragrance of incense flickered in the air. Rose breathed in deeply.

"How do you find these quirky places?"

"My travels. When I left you I just wandered and it led me to some amazing places. Let fear go, don't worry about getting lost and life will take you to some pretty awe inspiring places" Rose smiled.

Two servants came over and sat next to them. The food came and Rose was hand fed.

She couldn't stop laughing "I'm sorry I feel like a kid who's being hand fed by her mother"

"Let that barrier of thought down its because it's a new experience it's only natural for your cerebral thought to go back to the past. Just enjoy what is happening now not what happened in the past."

"Wait...about this past thinking Sebastian"

"Can we not talk about this now Rose" Sebastian raised his eyebrows and attitude drenched his voice.

"Okay, okay I'll stop"

After both had been hand fed, very little was said between each of them. They stood up and went out to the car, where Ralf stood waiting for them took them home. When they both got into the house Sebastian turned to Rose, who had her head bowed on to the kitchen work top,

"I'm sorry for what is about to happen Rose…"

"What are you talking about?"

Sebastian walked off into the bedroom and shut the door, Rose stood there stunned by these words racking her brain as to what he meant. She walked over to the settee turned the TV on and her eyes started closing. Her head-swaying heavy her thoughts drifted off and before she knew it, she had fallen asleep.

Dream2

She finds herself in the bathroom and turns to find a mirror in front of her, which reflects back at her infinity.

She touches the mirror and it's hard but as she lifts her arm her mirror image remains still. Rose looks away behind her and as she does the mirrors image reflects her arm lifting. She looks back to the mirror and then walks away but her image remains in the mirror. She sees stairs and walks down them but she's actually walking up them. She finds herself back at her bedroom and sees herself asleep. She walks over to touch her face and she wakes up.

INSANITY

How did I get into bed I can't remember?

Rose looked over to the side of her but Sebastian wasn't there, getting up she tip toed into the living room. Rose looked on as he scribbled on sheets of paper, he was throwing them to the side of himself. Surrounded by books and pads and papers all with writing and numbers on them, she looked horrified, slowly walking quietly behind him and trying not to stand on the paperwork. She whispered behind him

"Sebastian?"

He did not look up from the paper work. A book lay in front of him, she tilted her head to read it. The 'Voynich Manuscript' looked back at her.

Rose gasped and stumbled back it was the book that changed the view of the world and had an apparent hidden secret about life, she watched on trying to scream, to stop, but nothing came out. He carried on scribbling and in big letters, he wrote, 'I am you, you are me.'

Rose fell to her knees she put her hand out to touch his face but as she did Sebastian's body fell to his knees. "No Sebastian please…oh God no Sebastian please wake up."

Silence fell around the room and she saw the right hand grab a pen out of his left hand and put it down onto the floor. Rose rushed over to pick his body up but like stone she couldn't lift him. She lifted his head and sobbed.

"Sebastian what have you done"

Panic-stricken she looked around the room, the entire living room floor was covered with decrypted codes from the Voynich manuscript. She picked the script up quickly and flicked through the pages- her heart pounding in her head.

"Jesus, what have you seriously done Sebastian, you've tried to decrypt it all in one night."

Rose looked at his limp body and cried "please God Seb don't leave me, why have you done this to me why now?"

Choking on her sobs she raised his head in her hands and heavily kissed his cold lips.

"Jesus please help me now I need help what have I done"

Rose screamed from the top of her lungs

"Why now?"

Rose ran to the house phone and makes the call for an ambulance as she is on the phone she turns to find Sebastian stood behind her

"Shit, Seb you're okay?" She jumped back in surprise

Nearly dropping the phone as a tiny voice from the phone confirmed an ambulance is on its way now. Sebastian looked at Rose in a curious manner, touching her face as if he was seeing a human for the first time.

"Sebastian, you've tried to solve the Voynich manuscript, look at me, I am new to you now yes?"

Looking at her phased out he nodded gently. Nodding again gently he went to speak but nothing came out.

"The crypts are hypnotic Sebastian, that is your name.

Your memory is wiped clear of everything temporarily.

Before Rose could say another word, a knock on the door sounded and broke her train of thought.

"Hello it's the paramedics."

Running to the door she let them in.

"What's his name?"

"Sebastian, but I must warn you he won't talk."

They took blood samples and asked him to talk, but there was nothing. No expression or colour in his face.

"We will take him in for observation we need to do further tests would you mind coming with us?"

"No not at all" she looked on terrified.

"Please we will need further details about him and his past."

They carried his limp body to the ambulance that was waiting outside. Rose sat in the ambulance looking over him as he lay there seemingly asleep.

They arrived at the hospital and they were placed in a private room. With Sebastian, still sleeping the nurses took blood in silence. Rose watched as doctors came in and took his temperature and very little was said. She sat there by the side of him and gradually she nodded off on his bed.

Dream3.

She finds herself in the kitchen. A knife lies on the table. She picks it up and looks at the blade but there is no reflection. She drops the knife and backs in to a countertop. Scared and suffocating she sees Sebastian walk in to the kitchen. She speaks, but he blanks her, he is in slow motion but everything else is in fast motion.

A child slowly walks into the kitchen, Rose stops crying. She watches as Sebastian picks the child up and wipes its tears Rose asks,

"Who is this Sebastian?"

Sebastian looks at Rose directly, she stumbles backwards her hands slip on the counter top, and she looks at her hands to see blood dripping. She tries to wash her hands but it's not washing away.

In a daze the room folds over, and she's in her bedroom. Rose falls to the floor her hands are back to normal she quietly whispers, "what is going on?"

She looks to the bedroom door and sees Sebastian with the child saying.

"Don't ever stop asking questions".

The child asks why, and Sebastian says "because you'll find your answer".

They walk away Rose looks over and sees herself asleep and as she wakes up she looks to see Sebastian who is asleep by her side in the hospital.

Rose got up to go the bathroom and whispered to herself "never stop asking questions." As she looked down, she heard a voice reply.

"You'll find your answers" Rose stumbled back and looked around herself Rose whispered again.

"What is going on?"

a voice bellowed back, "good."

Rose jerked in her seat and opened her eyes immediately to find Sebastian still asleep. A hand was resting on her should and she looked up, it was a doctor

"Hello Rose may I talk to you for a moment?"

"Of course" she looked curious.

"We will talk in my office"

Rose followed her to a large office with walls of glass and blinds all around the room.

"Please take a seat"

Cautiously she took a seat in a black leather chair that reclined slightly.

"Thank you" she said quietly.

The doctor gathered some notes from the cabinet and sat down opposite Rose moving herself into the desk she continued. "I would like to start by saying thank you for bringing Sebastian to us; we have spent a lot of time finding him in the hope to helping him"

"I'm sorry what? Finding him? I'm sorry I'm a little confused I don't understand?" she shifted in her chair frustrated.

"I do apologise Rose, let me explain properly.

Sebastian has been a part of this hospital for a number of years now, he had a mental breakdown when he was younger.

It started when he was ten years of age I'm not sure if you know much about his past Rose…I shan't go on about it, but just to briefly tell you, he was readmitted again when he was twenty five years old."

Rose licked her lips and clenched her fists in disbelief.

"Wait hang on, he was sectioned?"

"Please let me explain further this will all make sense Rose. I am here to make light of the situation. Sebastian has what we call disassociation and has had this since he was a young boy. We have been led to believe he was hypnotised, as he can't remember as far back as the age of ten. A legal guardian would have had to have been with him. This caused a mental breakdown; we think a cheap semi professional did the hypnotherapy, as he is having episodes of trauma. Which means the hypnotherapy had been botched. His past, we are guessing had been traumatic and we have spent so many years trying to coax it from him."

Rose looked confused shaking her head in disbelief.

"I'm sorry I know it's a lot to process but I'm not finished. Sebastian is slowly coming out of his Psychosis- or hypnotherapy we think… we have had Ralf report back to us in regards to his development. He has a sense of detachment from reality and he feels no emotions at all."

Rose stood up,

"Wait wait, no that's not right, he has been having emotions, and feelings, he smiles and says he feels for me!"

The doctor backed her chair away from the desk and reclines back in it slightly.

"We believe that Sebastian has had emotions taught to him. He has mirrored them, almost like a psychopath does, and somehow the hypnotherapist has blocked the neurons to his amygdale and also the sections to his memory. We have been trying to stimulate the hippocampus, the cingulated gyrus, the thalamus the hypothalamus and epithalamus which are relevant to the processing of memories."

Rose sat back down, her face sullen.

"Why, why would someone do that to a child? I don't understand I mean, who took him to the therapist? Who was the therapist?"

"Listen Rose, we think that something traumatic happened and someone took him to block out the past to a certain extent. We can't undo what has been done, but what I have researched about hypnotherapy is that there is a pass code given to unlock the memories, we are unsure of this code or password given to him in his subconscious."

Rose stood up abruptly again pacing the room.

"Oh my God it all makes sense now…he has been acting strange, going to places that he can't remember how he got there, he has walked out of lectures with no explanation why. I have confronted him about his past and he has just deflected from it all." She smiles with excitement.

The doctor looked concerned, "Rose you must understand this is delicate situation, it's like he has lived a dream for many years with no emotional impact. He has been from one relationship to another with no thought or regards to other people's feelings.

He has copied people's facial expressions and spoke of emotions but he never feels anything his past has held him hostage from himself. Now his persona has been broken down and reality is seeping in, it's like waking from a deep sleep having a veil lifted from him."

"Yes yes he did speak of a veil."

"He will experience things like a new born child he will have immature moments and how he handles these emotions will be temperamental.

 He still hasn't been clear on his past."

"I understand...but subconsciously if the veil has been lifting won't his dreams tell him of what has happened?"

"We're hoping his dreams will reveal something, were hoping it is a bypass from the hypnotherapy he has had. Either that or he will open up to you, but remember Rose brace yourself and guard your own emotions he will look to you in a different light.

Your feelings for him have been true to yourself but Sebastian has been guarding himself, not through his own fault, but what he has said and done has all been a façade, it will be like teaching a baby about his emotion in an adult body"

Rose burst into tears she slowly and apprehensively reaches in her satchel.

"I must give you this," Rose pulled the Voynich manuscript out and gives it to the Dr who looked confused.

"What is this?"

"It's a very old manuscript that was founded by a Mr Voynich. He's tried to decrypt it, "but it's damn near impossible."

What does this have to do so Sebastian?"

"This may sound ridiculous to you, but he will have no idea who I am.

when he wakes up, it is said that if anyone decodes the book to find the formula and is under a certain star sign the forfeit is to lose your memory of your life, wiping everything that you have ever known and decrypted, only something so prolific will re-jog his entire memory back."

The doctor looked through her files quickly in an excited sense of something.

"Wait…how much of his memory will be re-jogged?

"Well.. all of it"

"My god!" The doctor stood up from her chair with haste." His memory has subconsciously tried to reset itself…it makes sense, he is trying to break through something, his curiosity is getting the better of his brain and is trying to override the foreign block on his memories."

Rose looked relieved

"So he's trying to break himself free? He knows something is wrong? However, he can't tell us because it's like an endless circle that repeats within his brain that brings him back to square one again, he has had to try to break from the repetitiveness by gaining access to other ways and the only way for that is to gain new knowledge from anything….or anyone? His brain is like a maze trying to find its way out of itself!"

The doctor looked to Rose with glee.

"Well he's trying to do our job, but I still think he is way off…there is something that will unlock his memories and I hope it's not going to be a long process.

"I understand it's a shock, he has said and done a lot of things that have come across as if he has hold of himself"

"Someone has taught him well over the years to deflect all human feelings, his past has dictated how he is now, but until we find out what has happened in his past we can't help him progress further and help him heal."

"So what do you want me to do? I have so much to think about I mean he isn't who I fell in love with and he's going to look at me differently and there are so many questions I want answering I mean…I just can't."

"Please Rose don't try to process all this at once it is mind boggling I know.

Rose felt her body wilt and her heart drop, her world had stopped and her mind was an uncontrollable mess. Shaking her head she gently wiped the tears from her raw skin and looked at the doctor she couldn't blink, she looked down to her knees and stood up.

"Thank you doctor I need time to just think."

"I'm so sorry Rose."

The doctor lent over to touch her shoulder, but she moved away, and walked towards the door, sobbing she pulled the handle down and walked out with no words. As she walked down the corridors of the hospital her mind numb her surroundings, she passed Sebastian's room in a daze. She watched as he lay there asleep, she walked in quietly and stood by the side of his bed. Taking his hand she kissed him, lent down and she whispered in his ear. She lent her forehead against his and walked away letting go of his hand.

Ralf stood outside the room.

"Hello Miss Banks, do you care for a ride or walk?"

"I'll ride thank you Ralf."

He opened the door and she dropped into the car closing the door after her she lowered her head into the car seat.

"Ralf?"

"Yes Miss Banks?"

"How come you never said anything to me about Sebastian?"

Ralf turned to Rose fully in the car and took his cap off

"I'm sorry miss banks, I was under strict oath to not say a single word it would have blown everything, the way Sebastian was with you was just amazing to see, and the fact that he had you on his mind for so long after your first departure was amazing to see just a glimpse of breakthrough.

" I got excited for him, and when he saw you I was dumbfounded I truly was…. Miss Banks you're the only one out of all of us even his closest friends to have touched a stone cold heart. And I have had to work with that for so many years it's been hard for me miss Banks trust me it's been like working with Jekyll and Hyde for years now.

He fights so hard with his demons, his past has just consumed him whole, the women whose hearts he has broken and the tears that have been shed for him have been ten folds, and I have had to drive every single one of these woman back with one single question that has always been asked....why? Yet I can't answer that for them not even to give them peace of mind. But with you miss banks, you have fought with him but understood him on so many levels, it's like you were made for him, cheesy as that sounds. No woman has stood by him for along as you have."

"So what do you think made him closer to me?"

"Your patience miss Banks, the lack of tears you have shed in front of him and the genuine love you have for him. Your anger your fear you hide from him, and that challenges him to show other sides to test you.

"I have heard him call you terrible names and you have persevered with him, and he is eternally grateful for that, you haven't turned away from him at his worst and you have loved him at his very best. You basically accept him for who he is, he is testing you because his parents failed him when he was younger."

"He is taking me through a rigorous test of Faith and patience, to make sure I'll never leave him?"

"Yes even through his worst times he wants to make sure you endure him on all sides of his personality, but I think even this situation now will test you miss Banks"

Ralf took her hands.

"But I beg for you to dig deep and understand his situation even though his past is still unknown"

"But Ralf he has never loved me? His emotions aren't real but are copied; he doesn't know who he is and its catch 22 what if after all I go through with him that his true persona doesn't like me for who I am?"

Ralf just stared at Rose and looked down.

"I'm sorry Miss Banks, that's a gamble you must take, sometimes you make life how you want it to be but in this case... He trailed off.

"Thank you Ralf."

She pulled her hands away from Ralf and sat back, her mind beginning to whirl again.

"I'll drive you home"

"Please."

Night had fallen and the streetlights hit Rose's eyes forcing her to close them tight. With each blink an image of Sebastian comes clear into her head of him lying there next to her. The smile that melted her, heart his voice that spoke such sweet adoring words had come from a copied soul, her heart felt heavy once again.

"Miss Banks we're here, are you okay?"

"Thank you Ralf I'm fine I just need time to think I'm sorry"

"Any problems please call me, Miss Banks"

Stepping from the car she walked towards her door. She pulled her keys out and put them into the door. Closing her eyes, she took a deep breath as a sharp image pops into her head again of them making love. His lips soft as he kisses her head after.

"Fuck"

She turned the key and walked inside. Rose stripped off and fell into her bed, she hugged the pillows that Sebastian had lay on and felt deceived. But there was a part of her that was understanding of this situation.

CHAMBER.

What is this utter monstrosity I feel within me? A devious sinful hate that consumes my soul. Where do I begin to understand such a mind numbing process of forgiveness.

My feelings flutter from one to another, my head in a spin and the emotions that flicker like a candle refusing to be blown clean out. With heavy breath I blow and darkness falls … Yet the smoke I inhale from the aftermath is choking and I'm seething from the anger from within.

Forgiveness is not easy, but the past I am yet to know…this will be a long and arduous journey. Do I walk along this path I have created or turn away from all I have known. To then be engulfed in sadness and self doubt, there is always a catch in life of whether I will regret what I have decided upon, it's a catch 22, would I feel like I have wasted my time either way?

Question marks come at me at great speed, something that cannot be answered until I've tried…at least I can say I have tried. I am somewhat in awe of my love, how he has coped well with everything but yet gone through life with such numbness and yet the disdain that drowns him. I have been there in his shoes so how can I walk away from something that I have been through? Would I like someone to walk away from me in my time of great and deep need? Now he has changed and the veil has lifted would he love me the same way as I do for him? The feelings unfold in me like a book that never ends. It is tiring and yet I have no control. Do I blank my own emotions to save myself from falling? It all comes down to me and me alone on this, there is a door shut within me am I willing to be open and see all that there is?

Rose closed her diary, tears fall like showers, lying awake for hours time stands still around her, she looks out to her window sitting in now a dark room, and she wiped her tears and fell to her pillow. Her eyes shut and blacks out.

Dream 4

She is sat on a bedroom floor and looks around herself, she is in a child's room "Hello?" She asks but the voice doesn't come from her it comes from the child stood behind her she is petrified and as she speaks again the child speaks.

"Who are you?"

"Why are you talking?"

"Why am I talking through you?"

Rose looks puzzled. Sebastian walks in "who you talking to?" The child stands there looking oblivious and Rose replies

"No one!" Sebastian looks bemused "okay go down and eat your food its ready."

The child runs off in slow motion and Sebastian remains standing. He looks outside, It's snowing he touches the window but there is no pane of glass in the frame. He lowers his head and walks off. Rose watches on as he walks right past her... she stands up and stumbles back.

She feels something in her throat so she swallows, it feels like food she then chews like she is eating and swallows again.

She walks up the stairs to find the child eating food and with each mouthful it eats, Rose eats as well. She cries and falls to her knees her face in her hands and shaking her head the room crumbles and falls away.

She finds herself at the foot of her bed watching herself sleep. Rose stands up and as she does she opens hers eyes and is encased in darkness.

She feels Sebastian by her side stumbling into the bathroom and turns the light on she looks in to the mirror but there is no reflection. Rose holds her head and spins to the floor. When Sebastian wakes up he picks her up and places her on the bed and walks away.

SEEING.

Rose was woken up by banging. She rubbed her eyes with a moan, got up and looked out of her window it was snowing. Dustbin men were trying not to slip as the snow fell heavy around them, a smile graced her face and she stretched. She looked down to the floor, there was a decision to be made today. Her smile faded to a concerned look and rubbing her face she walked away from the window and stripped off to shower.

As she stepped into the warmth that drenched her body she put her head back, and memories flashed through her like lightening of the times she spent in the shower with Sebastian.

Covering her face with her hands, she breathed deep, and remembered of how he brushed her face gently and kissed delicately around her body.

She sighed shaking her head away from her thoughts but they pounded through her. The look she would give him when they were making love, the infinity she saw through his eyes, in utter bliss as she lay next to him in his arms as he slept peacefully. She would watch him wondering what he was dreaming of however, that was a lie, he could not dream and never had but she missed the way he would kiss her neck to wake her up and whisper in her ear

"Good morning baby."

A smile and a peace from within would fall into place.

But all that was a veil. Her thoughts raced to anger and confusion and she faced the glass in the shower and rested her head against it. She closed her eyes tight, more thoughts beating into her skull of how he would be there for her in her hour of need, the things he had said to her "I love you, I need you, I'm lost without you, I love you to the moon and back"

The words hit her like stones. Her anger built up, not understanding how someone could be so cold towards their own child. what had Sebastian's parents been thinking. She thought.

Her hands turned to fists and her body shook, she growled gritted her teeth and pounded the glass hard with her fist.

She took one deep breath and with an almighty roar from within screamed, she pulled at the shower head and threw it to the floor.

Slamming open the shower door still soaking and naked she ran to the bedroom and smacked away a glass, which smashed into the wardrobe, screaming with intensity. She pulled her bedding off and threw it to the living room, she beat down on her bed, and threw her lamp across the room before kicking the bed.

Grabbing anything she threw it all against the wall, taking out her draws throwing them to the ground. She ran to the living room, and grabbing a vase with flowers that Sebastian had got her she threw it against the fire place shattering like her feelings.

Shards cutting into her bare flesh, she stood there out of breath taking one deep breath

"No" she screamed to the top of her lungs.

Her heart pounding as she walked to the kitchen she grabbed a knife and looked into the blade seeing her face, angered and pitiful reflecting back. She looks to her wrist, the words racing through her like a train,

"Don't do this"

"Do this it'll end all feeling."

"Stop now."

"Who needs you?"

Rose fell to the floor onto her knees exhausted from it all, frustration kicked in like a shock to the system. Looking at herself in the blade, tears dropped onto the tip…words hit at her, "what if?" Holding the knife close to her wrists she closed her eyes and images of her mother beating her whilst she was sleeping crept in. Rose would beg for her to stop and crying as each blow to her head hurt as bad as the next. Her mother dragging her off the bed throwing her to the floor, stamping on her wrists, screaming, her mother would grab her toys throwing them across her room, snapping all her figurines and shouting about how useless she was. Saying that she should have never been born, how she was a regret, how she wanted to kill her from day one, how she caused her pain in her life.

Rose would lie on the floor crying holding her wrists. Her mother would look down on her and spit on her face.

Stamping on her stomach, she would punch her legs and arms, grabbing anything she could to throw at Rose.

She found her strength to get up and try to move away from the shards that splintered the floor, but her mother would grab her by her neck seething into her face she would spit of how much she hated her. She wished her dead with all her might. Rose closed her eyes and opened them back in the kitchen.

She fell against the cabinet, the knife saws against her wrist cutting down into her veins, she bites her lip hard.

With a quick slice she did it again, she flipped the knife over to the other wrist, slicing through images of Sebastian in a loving embrace, kissing her face, running his fingers over her lips as he whispered how much he loved her, how she had changed his world.

Her already numb body, watching her blood run from her, a sigh of relief drifts from her body.

Her mind finally silenced, she lay down onto the cold kitchen floor and a whisper came from the inside.

"Wait…wait…wait…"a panic-stricken feeling forced its way through death that was approaching in a slow pace, she turned to see her blood run around her face she whispers to herself…

"I can't wait" a faint voice is heard from afar,

"Rose, please open the door," said a voice but Rose closed her eyes…

Dream 5

She is sat on a swing and Sebastian is stood next to her, the child is in a swing in the middle of them Rose asks,

"Where am I?" The child again speaks as Rose does.

Sebastian replies, "the park."

The child and Rose ask "Am I dreaming?"

Sebastian walks, looks at the child and kneels down. "You're not asking the right questions."

Rose goes to swear but nothing comes out vocally, Sebastian walks off and leaves the child on the swing. Rose follows and as she does, the child jumps off the swing and walks along side her.

"Where are we going?" Rose and the child shout.

Sebastian shouts back, "you'll see…"

As they all walk down a steep hill they find themselves in a bedroom with all sixties style interior.

The child opens the door and sees a woman hanging from the ceiling. Rose falls back stunned and covers her mouth. The child stands there staring at the hanged figure. Rose tries to move the child but it's cemented to the ground, as she pulls at the child it begins to crack and splinter. Rose stands back in shock and sees the child crumble like dust to the floor. She screams and Sebastian comes running up the stairs in slow motion to find the hanged body.

Rose touches Sebastian and he too cracks and shatters. She runs out the door into the forest. Lost, she falls into a pile of leaves, as she falls she sees a face buried in the floor.

She wipes the leaves away to find its her face, she screams "WAKE UP WAKE UP" but no voice comes out.

A tree falls from its roots in front of her and she's now standing at the foot of her bed again, she finds she's breathing a voice echoes from behind her.

"WAKE UP" Rose shunts back in bed and she looks out of the window. Its dark and cold.

AWAKENING FROM.

The hospital is hollowed with sleeping bodies and echoes of feet that run and walk from theatres to rooms of patients. Ralf looked up to see Rose still sleeping, he looked down at her wrists and breathed deep, he got up walked for a drink but as he opened the door a nurse approached him.

"Hello Ralf can I talk to you a second."

"Of course Marie"

"Let's go to my office"

Taking a seat Marie sits quietly by the side of Ralf. "How are you feeling?" she rubs his hand with comfort.

"Tired, shocked, just a lot at the moment"

"Of course, but we are here to help them both, you have helped us so much and we are forever grateful"

"Thank you" he smiled.

Marie took a deep breath and looked at Ralf, shifting closer to him.

"We have done tests on Rose we can't really determine anything until she is awake as we need to test her mental capability and get her version of events. You have given your statement to the police?"

"Yes"

Marie walked over to her desk and sits down.

"Ralf she has severe blood loss and is now in a coma, she has diabetes as well. Her glucose levels are dangerously low; it's what we call hypoglycaemia. Over time we will try something called a Glasgow coma scale, this level is monitored constantly for signs of improvement or deterioration."

Ralf buried his head in his hands, sobbing he shook his head..

"I know" Marie stroked her brow

"What should I do?" he asked in disbelief, his hope slowly fading.

"We will tell her when she's awake and fully functioning, her mind is blinded at the moment with everything that has happened."

"Of course"

"Ralf its okay don't worry we will keep an eye on her, but I suggest you just go back to your normal routine. I thank you for the time you have given us we will take it from here"

Ralf shoots a look at the window, it's snowing heavy and hard. He wipes the tears from his face and gets up from the chair, his legs like dead weights walked to Rose's room.

He kissed her hand gently and stroked her face whispering, "thank you Rose it was a privilege to know you." Walking from the room, he sobbed.

AWAKE.

Sebastian opened his eyes, shielding them away from the gleaming sun, he tried to get up but was bleeding still from his arm. He looked at it as if he couldn't remember how it happened.

Trying to remember anything he sat on the edge of the bed wondering what had occurred. He looked round the room with confusion, he got up slowly and looked out of the window, but as he stood his legs buckled from under him and he hit the floor hard. He opened his eyes and looked under the bed; there is a diary and he shuffles across the floor to reach It. He pulled it from under the bed and he lay against the bed to read it. He opens the diary to find diary pieces written by him he reads on…

DAMAGED.

I am mentally damaged in intricate depths and I believe I am intensely in love with someone. Whom I love, and whether I do or not is confusing to say the least, its best left in my head. As if, love is ever simple.

Simple love is in itself a complex thing. To simply love a person is to compress a deep and complex connection into simplicity, just because a

272

masterpiece is folded it does not mean there are not complexities hidden within.

To be in love is to navigate a complex thing easily, not to have it be simple. A simple thing can be solidly described and defined, something that poets and musicians have been trying to do since the dawn of time, all that can ever be said is "I love you" and trust the other understands and sees the great depth of feeling behind the words. People love differently, it is subtle but different, and your type of love is like your handwriting or your fingertips...unique to you.

To truly love another person is to navigate and understand their love for you with the same if not more ease then to navigate your own for them.

True love.....is two souls bound together.

Words are a failing catalyst towards my own self-destruction.

Sebastian put his diary down and stared at the words on the paper, he felt a welling up inside of him.

"Sadness" he whispered to himself, burying his head in his hands he soulfully sobbed. A nurse over heard him and came into his room and hugged him tight.

"It's okay Sebastian, we will help you through it all."

She took his diary.

"I'll take this to the therapy room, we will see you soon okay?"

He nodded slowly. Raising his heavy head he looked out to the window, leaves fell to the ground like his emotions, it was bright red and simply beautiful.

DREAM 6

Rose was stood in a river, the stream gently trickling around her feet; she looks on and sees the child stood naked in front of her.

Rose steps out of the river and as she does Sebastian comes over and gives the child a coat and picks it up, Rose watches on, the child sobs and Rose finds herself crying, tears roll from her eyes.

Sebastian speaks up, "where are your questions?"

Rose stands and thinks hard. "Where is mummy?"

"You know where she is"

"What is my name?"

"You know your name silly."

Rose could feel frustration. "Why am I outside naked?"

"Good" he says in a hopeful tone. "You sleep walk"

"Why do I feel sad?"

"You have had traumas"

"Why?"

"You know why"

Rose looked to one side. She whispered, "loaded questions"

"Speak up I can't hear you" he said frowning.

"Have you stopped beating mummy?" Rose said with a slight smirk on her face.

"Very clever" he smiled.

Another voice came from behind Sebastian; Rose looked shocked, as it was much deeper, quieter voice

"Have you stopped cheating on mummy?"

"You can't answer a question with another question I haven't got my answer!" Rose's anger could not be contained much longer.

"There are two of us."

Rose was in disbelief,

"No it's not fair they're loaded." As she looked down she had a gun in her hand

"You said it was loaded"

The child was holding a gun. Rose stood back, shocked she tripped and fell into her bed...she lay next to herself, shook her body and she woke up.

She whispered to herself "I'm getting there."

BELIEVE.

Sebastian entered the therapy room with caution.

"Please Sebastian take a seat settle in my name is Daniel do you remember me at all?"

"I'm taking it this will be a long session and no I don't remember you?"

"We have a lot to catch up on don't we?"

"A little"

"No a lot…"

"What do you care to know?"

"How are you?"

"I feel like I've come out of an extremely bad intense dream, newborn into a chaotic Veil free world"

"You're very lyrical"

"Sorry?"

"You're working and depth of perception has changed a lot, reading from your diary notes I have compared from before and after, there is a lot more emotion to your new entries"

"Yes, I'm trying to get to grips with that fact that I feel emotions now, it hasn't been easy unlocking them you know."

"What are you feeling now?"

"Fucking anger, for fucks sake! Why did you drag me out of something that I was happy in?"

"You mean your own mind numbing world?"

"Yes, that…now I have to confront this bullshit, and find out who I really am."

Daniel shifted in his chair uncomfortably

"Sebastian control yourself this is a healing process for you, it's like being a new born baby for you, trying to understand all that you feel and placing those feelings in the right situations in your life"

"What on God's earth are you talking about Daniel?"

"Sebastian, you have been withheld from yourself for so long, if someone says they love you, an emotion of frustration or anger may come into play where it is not needed, you need to sort your emotions into order."

"So basically I'm a fucking mess?"

"Not per say, no. We need to just monitor you because if we let you go now you will question yourself on a daily basis of whether the feeling is right for the moment you're in which will be extremely tiring and frustrating for you."

"Jesus what have I done?"

"This has been a delicate subject for some time now Sebastian...your past holds the key to who you are now that the veil has been lifted, we know nothing of your mother or father or where you have been for the past ten years..."

"So you're asking me, when I'm already at a delicate stage, what the hell happened to me when I was younger."

"Now is the best time"

"Don't talk to me about the now!"

"Okay, okay, I understand...today has been a long and tiring process for you, we shall leave it for today but these sessions will carry on till we feel you're safe to be alone."

"Fine, when can I see Rose please? Or is she visiting me?" Daniel shifted in his seat as if it became suddenly uncomfortable, he deflected the question.

"Look one last thing Sebastian, before you go, do you remember a book at all you were reading before you passed out, called the book of the Voynich Manuscript?"

"I remember a lot of things Daniel but it's a blur. I need to write it all down to straighten it all out in my head otherwise, it comes out like a jumbled mess.

 I remember reading a book yes not sure of the name, but I was scribbling manic things on there. I've asked for it all to be binned now"

"Well, Sebastian the book that you have read, it's a very medieval book that many people have tried to decipher and you tried to do it in one night"

"Really? What did it hold?"

"Something about eternal life? We're guessing something from your past has traumatised you in regards to death and you are subconsciously trying to survive death."

Sebastian looked to the floor and his mind shot back to the night he started the book many years ago, he had to go to the library to look at the thing, feeling the pages of vellum he was in awe, and made it his mission to unlock a mystery no one else could solve.

"Sebastian are you alright?" The daydream was broken.

"Yes something just came back to me now, what happened after I deciphered the book?"

"Your memory got wiped a little, sounds unreal but it's a very dangerous book."

"Sebastian fell back into his chair."

"So this is why I can't remember things? Because of a stupid book, and I was too busy trying to look for a formula for eternal life? What is wrong with me!

Looking over to his therapist, he smiles

"How are you feeling Seb?"

"Weird,"

"Your memory will return we hope through prolific events, something will jog your memory and everything will fall back into place, it'll take time."

Daniel smiled

"Thank you"

Daniel opened the door and Sebastian walked out of it slowly.

Turning back he said, "I will try my hardest to give you what you have wanted all these years but you have to thank Rose not me when it comes to the truth...." Daniel looked on puzzled.

"Of course, oh and one more thing before you leave...you'll notice when you sleep now Sebastian that you will dream, so please write down everything you remember because this will help to gain some insight into your past, the subconscious is a powerful tool"

"Will I have nightmares?"

"You may for a little while"

"How will I handle them?"

"You're in here safe with us. There is something called night terrors they're a lot more intense and realistic then normal dreaming but the nurses will be here to help you."

"Fuck, I dread to sleep…"

"You must or your Psychosis will reappear."

"That's what I'm hoping for."

"Now now…"

Sebastian sighed and turned away. He made his way to his bedroom when a sudden flash of thought took him and he fell against the wall.

SEBASTIANS PSYCHOSIS EPISODE.

I put my books away and I stare to the window my mind blank, I get up thinking if I walk so many steps I'll drop dead, I shake the maddening thought from my head and continue walking upstairs, I feel light and interrupted, I have visions flicking through my mind like a TV.

I see my phone and I make mad ranting phone calls to friends stating "I am you, you are me" and thanking them which was a statement of I am everywhere as if it was a pass code, hoping I'll pass to the dark side. A veil I feel has come between me and reality, I put the phone down from friends feeling I am accomplishing life's work. I have an aim in life...to see the future and warn people of the dangers ahead.

I dress in black and walk to work in a daze no other thoughts come, but that people are demons. I am a good will at work, to me there is no time, just space.

My thoughts flicker to absurdity coming and going, my mother hanging herself, my friends raping me, my family against me...I believe every thought I felt every emotion.

I'm back home...how did I get here? I state to my friend, I am on the other side they should join me its peace and tranquillity. He looks beyond worried. I fear someone's out to kill me. I know a dark and deep seeded secret that many elite members of a secret underground society try to keep hidden. Cars come and go and I grip for my life, I explain my captions "you are me I am you thank you."

Transcended beyond and I am nothing. I have manuscripts that have failed to be decoded by the most brilliant minds from round the world, and I crack each one over night in utter awe of secrets that pour from the manuscripts.

Being nothing was peaceful, but reality kept penetrating my thoughts, mixing my emotions...

I awake ...I think I've slept, I think I've eaten, I think I've showered. Water was poison and swallowing my own saliva was in my mind. Alcohol. I hadn't slept for a week breaking codes and finding the universe's secrets and pasts untold and unfolded in my very hands.

I only ate biscuits and drank milk, my appetite had gone, but I kept going.

I sit there gravity holding me in place. my visions of madness intensified, my eating diminishes, humans become intolerable and I lose my bearings I forgot who I was...my thoughts not my own but now of something else. Simple questions from the doctors became unbearable, now unable to think the veil between reality and nothingness thickens. Nurses asking to take blood. My mind was casted back to a crack den, injecting heroin, I'd fall to the waste side, the nurse-my dealer...I pull back my arm crying, her soothing voice from reality seeped through. She took my blood, and I've been injected with heroin, I sit in silence as I waited for the feeling to kick in...nothing, it was not real, my friend sat by me crying nervous.

I ask calmly "why so afraid?"

I finally get given a hospital bed, urine sample needed...it was dark orange. I began to panic, the nurses needing to calm me, I sat looking at words that made no sense on a hospital bin. My mind not letting go..."pen" I scribble words...pass codes pass secrets...the doctors look at me in disbelief that this had been induced purely by me alone and no narcotics. I could swear I have cancer, no Ebola, no every illness under the sun.

DSM.IV.TR needs abolishing mental illnesses are of one thing ...thoughts.

Diagnosing myself at an alarming rate, have I breathed? I take deep breaths wait...am I dead?

I look to the mirror and I see sunken skin and black eyes, bad yellow rotting teeth...my father's face staring back at me.

283

I fall away, doctors come and go...I declare I've been raped, hurt, molested, I write every partner I have had down on paper and making connections. Coincidences of the same name and surname like a never ending loop of madness ...I declare doctors have raped me, I grab my friends phone shouting some ones going to die, even though I now realise the phone was switched off. I'm calmed by my friend, I sit staring into thin air, my mind talks on my behalf now, I say nothing I am silenced.

I think I am speaking aloud when I am really saying nothing...I stare to the open window what is this I feel? I cannot see it yet it makes me cold "air" my mind whisper, but my friend sees me looking confused.

Nightfall's but my mind thinks it's daytime. Sleeping tablets are given and I grasp my friends hand as if it is my last breath and I sleep.

The next day I am awakened by noise. I am still here alive. I am asked if I want to go to a psychiatric ward...I agree, still in my mind I may kill or be killed. I'm walking slow and with caution but my friend pushes me to move faster. My head spins...am I alive. I wake up I'm been driven to the ward, the car stops and I'm congratulated for getting this far.

I gather my belongings and walk through the halls, the smell of flowers is overwhelming, the colours of reality are bright almost three dimnesional.

A friendly face, a warm smile, greets me, he talks of the here and now and I kiss his hand. I am shown my room and my friend sits with me....staring and crying at me, I think, why so sad? A doctor enters and he asks me to spell WORLDWIDE WEB backwards.

I recite with no failure the entire sentence backwards in a split second. The doctor looks stunned, he turns to my friend.

"Is he normally this quick?" My friend looks astonished.

"No he can't even string a proper paragraph together so this is new to me." The doctor states it's clever, and warns me my mind is working at an alarming rate.

I cannot control the speed of my thoughts, I draw boxes for the doctor to see if I perceive correctly...I fail and he leaves the room.

My friend gives me music to listen to and we depart until another day. I have pen and paper and I'm writing the lyrics down at speed never having to pause the music...I write furthermore in a manic fashion, confessing of my sins wondering what I had done in the past to have me turn this way...what secrets had I not been told? What is my unconscious mind keeping me from?

I looked out of my window to see a church. "My mother's dead" I whisper. In the chapel of rest..."I'll see her tomorrow" I rest my head looking at the floor my mind in a panic thinking I was in a gas chamber I don't fight any more, I'm exhausted I rest my eyes and cave in.

Another day arrives I awake to the sound of a patient singing aloud, I now have no concept of days I have lost all time. I look at my body and wonder what to do. I look at the sink in my room...my mind slowly piecing together "wash" I wash..."clean teeth" I clean my teeth. I feel bowel movements..."what is this?" "toilet" the list was endless "dress" ..."make up"..."hair"..."food"..."eat"..."walk"..."breath"...It became tiring. I began sleeping better at night.

My mind slowly coming to reality, my veil lifts. My friends remind me of laughter, sadness, sex, I am unaware of my male form. When they left I touched between my legs, I feel pleasure as I run my hand up and down myself. I put my head back and continue to feel happiness, but stop. My door is unlocked and I am getting tired, another day maybe.

I wake and it's daylight its Sunday. I hear screaming its six in the morning but the girl opposite me has sunk deep in her mind.

Throwing and stiffening her body I watch on as everyone is ushered to their rooms...have I done this to her?

I am still unwell, her head is thrown back and forth and her screams penetrate my very bones. I stand in awe of how the mind controls all we see.

The way we perceive and behave, she scratches herself and blood is pouring, she grabs at her mouth as if to break her jaw, the nurses and doctors try to restrain her as she fights them off clawing at their faces.

A needle is injected, six men hold her tiny frame of a body down to the bed her body bruised and bleeding, flesh torn, I stand shaking my head in disbelief.

"What have I done?"

I am human I never chose to be born...I can turn like that any time and we have no control of any outcome. I feel anger I feel my soul collapsing I sob so hard that I cannot breathe I grab my bed sheets in both hands where I sit and cry a painful thought.

I cannot end my life...I cannot end my life...I sob harder my chest and the pit of my stomach hurt.

I am to live with such sadness and I do not have the guts to kill myself.

I am stuck here...I am to live with such madness and I can't come away from my thoughts.

My door is thrown open, a girl stands there my crying immediately stops and I wipe my tears away quick, thoughts of suicide extinguished I am now overwhelmed with curiosity. I follow the girl into a room of doctors and I sit down....

"Mr Lawrence" I look around myself wondering who he's talking to.

"You have shown improvement ....one question though do you know who you are?" my face looks confused, my mind throws me back.

I had lost my identity, I was thinking I was everyone and everything, I thought I was my mum my dad my doctors but I was never me. The doctors explained I had been in hospital for over a month I was losing concept of reality forgetting people and never recognising who I was. I sit there back in the room. I need out of this ward. My mind screams at me to speak, speak...

I speak the words, "I am Sebastian Lawrence" the doctors looked happy...

Sebastian awoke to find himself back in his hospital bed. He sat himself up slowly and blinked taking a sip of water. He turned his lamp on, looked under his bed, grabbed his diary, and began writing.

CLARIFYING.

Reassessing myself and looking at those I play with, their feelings fray at the stem. I begin to see we're all desperate for love and want, there will be ones that fall, anger, or accept, but rarely those that will forgive.

The memories within ourselves are torture devices, just as we forgive a jog of memory folds back to how we felt the first time we hurt. Bitterness sways our deciding time and when everything falls apart it'll eventually come together. It's a clarifying thought.

My bitterness and hatred stems from my childhood everyone's problems do. Mine was loveless again a cliché for every human whose parents back in the day did not have what we have now and we suffer the consequences.

 We're made to put the past behind us and move on but this unfortunate thing called memory creeps in like a unwelcome friend and shows us the past like a film on repeat. Each time we view this our feelings either bear it or fear it, depending on our mood in that moment.

I however prove to have bitterness; things my mum said resonate strong within me. Out to prove her sadistic ways wrong I ruin and wreck people's feelings I turn to the vulnerable and play with them to then walk away knowing they feel how I feel.

It is a wretched thing to do, but my anger has consumed me and as I look back all I see is black where my past has been.

All that is left is the feeling and an emotion so strong is wells up like the Pacific Ocean drowning out my sane thoughts taking out every sensation of love and compassion I have in my bones. I hate, I loathe, I have no regrets and those that walk away from me with their heart intact, lie… I need to break, shatter, splinter, every soul I see in sight. Those who are nice to me I break down until they turn to God. I know there isn't one. They can only turn to themselves which is a regret as they are not as they were. Their minds broken, and their thoughts come in like a tidal wave taking away forgiveness and love and I stand there with a smile of happiness amongst their misery. Hell hath no fury but I am not scorned.

I am merely just a walking bag of bones entwined with a sense of moving forward through days.

Each day and night I am hoping it is my last. I am weak for not taking my own life … but there is reason that I'm trying to find and it gets smaller and smaller with each passing second. My temper greys at the thought of why, which then turns to boredom and inevitably turns to harm.

The human form is too easy to dismantle, the brain easy to disconnect, words are everything and the feeling comes in like a blast from the past I stand back as there is chaos with no theory.

I watch on in fascination as I see emotions pelt from their very souls. Tears torn from their heart, and head sadness rips through their bones and I stand and I glare as they choke on their tears. Breathing impaired and their hands to their faces their body weeps like a willow. I turn away in utter dispute of their emotions, why can't I feel their pain? Their sorrow? Their breaking of a heart and soul? Jealousy swamps me and a cycle starts again of anger to which I find is now never ending. Who can finish this?

Me! I hear my mind whisper, the reminder of suicide is like a constant friend in need. Death isn't to be loved or cared for but a life is….and it would carry on without me. If my bones were to be turned to ashes the ground will be the only thing to welcome me…or would it?

Giving chances hasn't been a thing for me, I've taken enough. Too afraid to give for fear of rejection, too young to understand I would find myself alone, those that cared to love me I would question their judgement of me.

I am self-loathing, no one to harm but myself, safe in my own thoughts…until now. Rose, Rose, how you have broken me free from my shackles that burrowed deep into my flesh like the thoughts that penetrate. My hate that turned to love, that shone so bright, I turned away. A new feeling that my body accepted. Who are you?

My life my soul, my love, mine. Accepting all that I am. Is this my saviour I see? Do I finally love?

Sebastian put his diary away with a feeling of happiness which is new to him. He smiled with a sincere look, walked to the mirror to see his face and saw the smile was natural. He looked to his bed and his eyes felt heavy, he rested his head on his pillow and drifted off.

BREAK FROM THE PAST

The curtains were whipped open and a nurse rudely barges through the door, slamming around the ward.

"Awake Mr Lawrence? The therapist wants to see you now."

Only just coming to the bright light that penetrated his eyes, he glared up at the nurse

"Why so abrupt?" He asked in a sleepy tone...

"The therapist needs you now please dress quickly he's down the hall to the left"

"Ummm okay?"

Sebastian pulled his legs from the bed a worried feeling hit him hard, thoughts go through his head and he feared he had been proven wrong...

He closed his curtains, got dressed, and walked slowly towards the office, he heared other people in the room and stepped back from the door.

"Mr Lawrence I can see you outside please come in," the therapist shouted from inside the room. Sebastian walked in to find two men sat there smartly dressed and his therapist looking unshaven and tired.

"Nice to finally need you Mr Lawrence my name is Jacob I am here to help you through your process today as it will be ripped from your memory"

"What the fuck is this?"

"Mr Lawrence please take a seat"

He sat quietly but with a worried look on his face…

"Mr Lawrence, you have been in a Psychosis for some time now since the age of ten your feelings and emotions shunned all by you and you alone…do you understand?"

"Yes I do?"

"It's a quick process Mr Lawrence what that has taken years to gently coax and prod from you we can now do today in one fell swoop."

"How?"

"By telling the truth Mr Lawrence…we have read your recent diary entries, and it shows you're fully out of your Psychosis but your emotions and feelings are yet to be brought into line. This will take time and after this session I will have the nurses medicate you so you cope well with what's happened."

"I don't understand how are you going to do this?"

"How much are you willing to pull yourself apart now Mr Lawrence to find your past that you have denied for so long? You hold back your past you fear to face it but if we give you something called Pentothal we could help you face the truth."

"What?"

"Basically truth serum."

"Wow umm I don't know, I've only ever seen it in movies I didn't know it actually existed?"

"Yes it's hardly ever used but I fear that death will take you before we can help you Mr Lawrence we have been up all night debating this and we care for your safety but when this serum wears off you won't remember what you have said so we will record this session"

Sebastian sat back on his seat and took a deep breath...

"Well I knew this was going to come for sometime the truth will have to be told I need to do this but do I have to hear the recording after?"

"If you like it's up to you, personally we would like you to listen to it and see if it does re-jog anything else?"

"Can't you just wait for my dreams to tell me something?"

"Sorry but your dreams are not accurate enough and that could take years plus they will be utter nightmare and without help they will harm you personally"

"Okay, well... Let's do this."

The therapists sat there stunned a look of amazement on their faces.

"Please Mr Lawrence lie down on the couch, and rest your body"

Nervous, he stood shaking, lay down and closed his eyes.

"Don't sleep Mr Lawrence we need you fully awake and conscious you'll feel a little pinch and then cold liquid it takes 5 minutes to run its course through your body."

"I'm feeling...nervous like a sick feeling"

"Don't worry that's normal"

The needle inserted and Sebastian jumped a little he felt a cold feeling in his arm and then he felt calm.

The therapist stepped back and cleared his things away and took a seat on the far side of the room.

"Okay Sebastian how are you feeling?"

"I think umm calm like woozy."

"A dreamy euphoric feeling will come into play...let me know when you feel a rush of warmth and we will begin."

Ten minutes passed and Sebastian tried to sit up but he fell back down onto the seat

"Yeah that was a warm feeling"

"Ok we will begin as long as you're comfortable because it could take a while"

"Yes I'm fine"

"Alright"

The sound ofthe recording began.

"So Sebastian when you were ten years old you witnessed something dramatic something so prolific it stopped you in your tracks is this correct?"

"Well I guess so?"

The therapists looked at one another.

"So what exactly had happened that day or night that made you shun your emotions?"

"I....I.....I" he got a slow and painful shock from his left temple. He sat up putting his head in his hands.

A voice come pounding in from the side; he held his head harder digging his nails in to his scalp and closed his eyes tight as if he was waiting for something to hit him hard. A voice bellowed from afar but too far for it to make any sense.

A shock hit his chest like a meteorite and he fell back on the settee, his face shocked at the feeling. His eyes sprang open to see his mother in front of him her eyes black as night; in a flowing gown of red so deep that it looked like blood. A passion of wind hit his face.

He is frozen to the spot and he cannot move his body, he watched as she came over to his left ear, he is petrified; the ground is heavy beneath him as if he is going to cave in. She whispers.

"FEEL"

Her voice is like a long-winded echo, there is a sharp pain in his ear, he closed his

eyes tight with a feeling as if he had been hit on the back of his head, his neurons pulsated and a flow of energy fell through his body shocks are sent through his cerebral synapses a bright light is shone.

Sebastian's memory flashed back so quick that he curled up into a tiny ball on the sofa. One of the therapists was about to stand up to sooth him but he sat back down when he saw Sebastian unfurl himself slowly.

SEBASTIAN'S PAST

My hand clutched the cupboard door shut. I hear screaming, crying…the two titans of my life railing against each other with the roar below of a sky gone to storm, the other a shrieking banshëe wail the likes of which only men hear when in grips of a hurricane.

Then finally manic laughter the laughter that chills to the bones and further still tearing into your soul with claws of cold iron.

The abrupt end, the snap of crushing gristle, fractured bone and a gurgle as a last laugh at the world around her. Some sounds of struggling, choking and gagging then the sound of arms falling at the hopeless weight of inevitable death and stillness. Is it safe?

My hands tighten round the door knob probably not. I should wait, I should. The door is torn open and the demon appears gripping my neck in its vice like grip and pulling me in.

"You see this, boy? This is what happens to sinners; they give into their inevitable destruction and end their own life!"

He leans in closer the stench of enough alcohol to set a man's blood on fire pressed into my face, "you're next boy!"

He laughs and flicks his eyes around he sees the shot gun upon the wall and drags my mother's helpless corpse around by the trail on her dark red dress

He drops me in a heap onto the floor and walks to the gun.

I see his head twitching involuntarily, I look up and I see my mother now held by her neck with his hands her face twisted and wrists cut with her crooked neck slanted to one side. A large stain spreading from her crotch began to appear through her dress.

A slight grasp to my left made me look again upon my father, holding the gun in his hand loosely and staring at his wife held high above the ground as if he was ready to let her go off the balcony. Her dress was flowing in the wind.

His legs gave away and he began to mutter to himself his knees struck the polished wooden floor and he gazed at her and then the gun. He looks up at me, my emotions hidden behind a practised mask a slight smile.

"I'm sorry lad"

Then he raised the gun to his head and a loud crack splits the air. Fragments of skull and brains, blood and flesh spatter the walls and me.

I pause…staring at the mutilated corpses. He let go of mum as he fell to the floor I hear her falling through the air, her dress snags on a pole. I run towards the edge screaming, the wind hitting my face it takes my breath away I hear more cracking of bones as she is hung by her dress.

She is flailing against the side of the building blown around in the wind like a rag doll. I close my eyes tight…is it safe? No, it is never safe! Never again… I hear sirens from afar I sit crossed legged onto the floor, showered in my father's blood a baptism of sorts I smiled at the thought; well they always wanted me to believe in their God.

Sebastian was staring at the ceiling as silence fell round the room; he looked towards the therapist and whispered, "people don't remember paragraphs that define everything they are trying to say. They don't remember a detailed description of your soul laid into neat lines organised with correct punctuation."

They remember that which hypnotises them with the complexity of the feeling they remember who they feel."

The therapists sat there blinking at one another rubbing their faces and looking gravely concerned.

"Mr Lawrence I think we have progressed far enough for today I thank you so much for your time."

Sebastian lay there with a bewildered look on his face. "Have I done well?"

The therapist smiled at Sebastian and rubbed his hand.

"Yes Sebastian you have done well thank you the nurse will take you to your room and sedate you whilst you come back from the serum."

The nurse entered the room quietly and gently, helping Sebastian up from the sofa. As the door shut behind him the therapists took a deep breath and sighed. Daniel faced the other doctors in the room with case notes scribbled far off the page.

"We will continue on tomorrow"

The day's rolled by and Sebastian was continually put under the serum...each day was as harrowing as the last.

Therapy 2: His father beats him made his mother watch as he bled from every orifice. His father had Jekyll and Hyde syndrome he repeatedly raped his mother keeping the door open so he could hear the screams.

Therapy 3: His father would beat him if he cried; smiled, laughed, or showed any forms of emotions or feeling. He would witness his father taking other woman, as his mother would be forced to watch.

Therapy 4: He was left in a child hostel where he was tormented watching other girls being raped and killed. He was taken into therapy sessions until his father was free to take him home.

Therapy 5: Sebastian admits being in and out of hostels after his parents died. He was sent to a doctors office who began talking to him about his past. He began by asking for Sebastian to close his eyes, then after a while Seb realised he had no emotion. He thought he had just grown numb to the world around him. When he says he loves someone he never feels it he feels it's a normal thing to say because that's what woman liked to hear in the movies he would watch on loop.

Each day that passed by Sebastian confessed to more horrific stories Daniel got more and more concerned if Sebastian should ever listen to the tapes, in fear that he will traumatise him of sorts. Daniel asked a nurse to call Mr Lawrence in his office.

A knock on the door and he called him in.

"Please Mr Lawrence take a seat. As you know you have told me of your past in great details and you have handled the comedown well after each session"

"Thank you Daniel it's been good to get it off my chest for some reason I feel lighter mentally after each session."

"Good to hear Mr Lawrence, I will keep your recordings as you seem to be progressing a lot faster than we would normally expect and we are wanting to release you from the hospital soon."

"Good I'm happy to hear that, so what to do now?" He said in a hopeful tone

Daniel stood up and walked to his window staring out amongst the tall buildings.

"There are other things that I don't want to talk to you about yet, there will be a few more sessions yet and I don't want any setbacks. You're in a very fragile position at the moment."

Sebastian nodded, "yeah that's fine"

He walked back to his room.

Night fell around Sebastian's room he lay there head burrowing his head into the pillow confused as to how he felt. Anger? Sadness? Frustrated? He felt his eyes heavy and he drifted off into a sleep.

Dream 7

Rose is standing in the rain in a deserted street, absolutely drenched she looked up to a house, which has a light on, and a blind closed.

She looks closer, walking over the road she can see shadows.

"No."

She runs to the house and bangs on the door screaming but no voice comes out. She looks behind herself, there stood the child.

"How can I get in?"

The child said in her voice again and it pointed to the left and Rose ran to the back and unlatches the door. She ran upstairs but as she ran, gravity pulled her back.

"NO"

Rose screams but nothing is coming out. She stops and sees that the child has hold of her foot so she slaps the hand away.

Rose runs into the room and slams the door open, there taking her last breath lies Sebastian's mum. A final struggle and her neck snapped and silence fell. Rose fell to her knees and looking behind the body Sebastian stands there watching out of the window

"Where are your questions?"

"Why did you kill your mother?"

"Did I?"

The room flips and Rose is stood opposite Sebastian the room spins around them both and out steps Sebastian's father. He speaks in a jittered voice

"You mentioned loaded questions!"

Rose looks down and sees a gun in her hand but she cannot not move Sebastian raised the gun to his father's head and Seb's dad raises his gun at Rose's head. Her heart is beating fast.

"Ask questions Rose."

Sebastian's dad raised his voice "You'll find answers"

Rose panicked, her eyes darting around the room.

"Have you finished killing your father Sebastian?" Sebastian and his father smiled at each other.

 The room spins as Rose is lead into a room where she sees Sebastian hanging his mother and then the room spins back to Seb pointing the gun at his dad's head and he at Rose, Rose screams.

"Wake up!"

Rose closes her eyes and falls to the floor, as does Sebastian and his father ran to grab her, she screamed.

"Wake up wake up wake up."

Sebastian awoke sweating and panting he looked over and saw it was dark outside, he looked at his hands nothing in them no gun no blood, and he looked round his room and got his bearings. He walked to the bathroom and put cold water over his hot face

"What a blissful feeling."

He returned to bed still shaken from the dream and wondered what he had said in his sessions. He needed to clarify his dreams to see if any of them were true. He lay there thinking hard as to what to do. Curiosity surrounded him and he wanted to know what was going on once and for all…

He waited until night fall when the ward was quieter. The ward creaked and only a few footsteps could be heard, Sebastian popped his head from round his door and crept to the reception area, there sat a plump lady eating grapes.

"I'm ever so sorry to bother you, but I'm wondering if I can get something to eat I'm a little hungry and I don't know where the kitchen is?"

"Oh okay what room are you in and I'll bring you your food Mr…?

"Oh Mr Lawrence in room sixty."

"Okay brilliant I shan't be long"

As the receptionist walked off he looked over her desk, under it lay the keys to all the offices in the hospital. He ran around the desk looking for cameras

Fuck it he thought. He quickly glanced over the keys to find Daniels office and he grabbed them. He ran to the next floor, adrenaline filled his body, his heart pounding he smiled as he ran to the office watching round corners for any doctor or nurses. He looked at his watch, 5.59am flashed back at him. "Okay I've got to do this quickly." he whispered to himself as he came to the door of Dr Daniel Ranson,

He stood there staring at the door his hand shaking. His brain screamed to just unlock the door whilst his heart hid in the shadows. But he saw a glimpse of light at the end of a tormented tunnel he fell against the wall, a sharp clear image crashed his thoughts; a gun held to a blanked out face. his heart racing his skin clammy, a vision of the book passages flicked through his head.

"Fear not, for what you don't know never hurts until the truth is revealed…

Sebastian slid down the wall, his head in his hands shaking, he can't.

Crying he looked up to the ceiling and whispered, "thank you."

A strange vivid feeling of panic struck his body accompanied by a sudden flash back of a room and his mum standing still with her hands held out. Her wrists are cut and bleeding.

He shut his eyes tight and closed his ears; suddenly he felt a tap on his shoulder and jumped up, but nobody was there. He looked around panicked before facing the door again. He put the keys in, he was inside. Looking in the dark, he felt along the wall for a light switch finally finding one he squinted as the brightness hurt his eyes. He looked around the room to find a filing cabinet with two locks on them.

"Shit shit shit you stupid idiot they're all locked!"

He looked down at his keys and rushed to lock the door behind him so no one would follow. He noticed out of the corner of his eye there were the filing cabinet keys. Hoping to himself they were the right ones to unlock he nervously put the keys into the cabinet. A smile sprinted across his face and rush of relief drowned him as they turned and unlocked the drawer.

He flicked down the alphabet to find his name, his hands shaking uncontrollably he had to stop and just calm himself down.

He breathed deep and tired again, there before him was his file he threw it to the floor and unlocked other cabinets to find Rose's. Finally he held his hands the files and answers he has been wanting for so long. Trying to control himself; he took a seat at the desk and opened his file finding his recordings that dropped out over the floor.

He knelt down to pick them up; under his desk he found the recorder.

"Well it's like something wants me to find the truth." He muttered to himself. He took the recorder and put it on the desk and he started to read his case file...

CASE FILES.

Mr Sebastian Rowling Lawrence

Born: March 24th 1977

Age: 38

Place of birth: London

Mr Lawrence brought in June 1st 1982 with stab wounds to his arms and legs at the age of ten with severe trauma.

No speech and no eating.

Possible schizophrenic episode.

Therapy session very little said only mumbling of which we cannot get a word of. To be kept in a Psychosis ward for further analysis.

Escaped the ward 14th June 1982- on high alert police out to find him.

15th June 1982: Found wondering the street, brought in by a couple concerned for his safety, and seeing wounds.

Continuous therapy sessions has now been on the ward for nearly fifteen years eating has come with positivity still no speech and no further progress with his past. Mr Lawrence is making progress we find through his psychological experiments that he has been hypnotised. This is blocking certain memories, possible therapy done by a number of hostels he has attended.

He sighs a lot sleeps very little doesn't dream at all no REM no recollection of what he had done the day before…no emotion or feeling.

Conclusion: Hypnotism acting as psychosis from trauma.

Sebastian looked over his arms to find stabbing scars, he looked shocked he had never seen them before now. He looked down his legs long dragging scars of stab wounds over the back and front.

"Why have I not seen these before?" He whispered.

Running his fingers over his scars he had a flash back of him running down the stairs grabbing a knife and just ploughing it into himself. He could feel nothing. He wept, sobbed as he saw the blood drain from his body. Sebastian gulped for air and grabbed the desk, the visions were as clear as daylight. He breathed deep and grasped at the file to look further on…

Mr Lawrence has been admitted with withdrawal from Psychosis/hypnotherapy after escaping from our hospital.

New case file 66:

Mr Sebastian Rowling Lawrence

Born: March 24th 1977

Place of birth: London

Mr Lawrence admitted to our hospital 6th June 2015 along with his girlfriend Rose Banks.

Has been reading a hypnotic book claiming he can find the key to eternal life...

He is talking and eating with no problem but his emotions and feelings are slowly unfolding. Under observation until further notice.

Mr Lawrence escaped the ward.

Breaking and entering.

Mr Lawrence is under investigation by Daniel Ranson, an undercover police officer.

Sebastian fell back from his chair his body riddled with guilt his eyes darting back and forth

"No no no no this can't be true, not any of it… No it's a lie all of it"

He stood back from his case file looking at it in disdain and hate he kicked the table and anger swirled his body

"Shit Rose…"

He went back and quickly opened her case file.

Case file 666:

Case file of the children's hospital of London Chelsea poison control centre:

The use of carnitine for the management of acute valproic acid toxicity

Miss Rose Faith banks

Born March 26th 1988

Age:29

Place of birth: London, Chelsea

A ten year old white female was found unresponsive outside of her home at around six o' clock in the morning. She was witnessed to be awake twelve hours beforehand then shouting and screaming...

A passerby was unable to wake the patient and called Emergency medical services (EMS) there is no history of headache or dizziness, fever, chills, nausea or vomiting seizures

We found a concerning amount of Valproic acid in Miss Banks body, suicide attempts have been noticed on her body reports, the valproic is used for neurological and psychological conditions.

Miss Banks is now responsive   and doing well, eating has come back but is kept under suicide watch; therapy sessions are ongoing, she would not tell us if it was her or another person who gave her the drug.

Unfortunately there are hallucinations that comes with Miss Banks, any traumatic event is reconstructed in her mind as an event not as traumatic, and will envision herself doing the traumatic events that occurred.

We have found that her father died of an overdose when Miss Banks was only 5yrs old and her mother died in hospital from a cardiac arrest.

There have been cases brought forward for Miss Banks of severe beatings and abuse by the hands of her mother Miss Hope Banks.

Miss Rose banks has been released from the ward with ongoing therapy sessions she must return to on a regular basis if this is breeched she will be put under psych ward watch again.

Sebastian read on with his heart beating hard...

Case file 616:

Miss banks readmitted 6 June 2015 with slash wounds found on her wrists body beaten, broken left wrist and cracked skull with severe bleeding further investigation found Miss Rose Banks three months pregnant but the foetus is growing at a slow rate admitted by her side was a Mr Sebastian Rowing Lawrence, who had escaped the hospital.

Sebastian was in shock. His jaw dropped and his face paled.

"She's pregnant" he whispered "she's here in the hospital!!" He was relieved because he could see her but concerned at the same time he felt sick and concerned. His body shook and was wondered why she had tried to kill herself. He moved her file to one side and a police case dropped out he knelt down to see it was Rose's…

Case file 616 of Rose Faith Banks:

The police and ambulance were called after there had been a disturbance at the Lawrence's residence. Their chauffeur heard the fight and tried to gain entry to the apartment but with no avail so called authority to the site.

The door was broken open to find a Miss Rose Banks on the floor naked with her wrists slashed and bleeding heavily. Mr Lawrence was knelt by her side holding a knife and shaking muttering uncontrollably showing bruises across his arms and face. On searching the apartment, the bedroom was badly damaged showing signs of struggle. Both Mr Lawrence and Miss Banks are under investigation.

Sebastian sat there stunned, his body stiff and unable to respond, he blinked.

"What the….no fucking way had I done that to her? I had been in…."

His head hurt and a flash back hit him. He had escaped the hospital to find Rose, his vision and thoughts was blurred misinterpreted. He had got into a taxi, which he ran from and entered the house in the morning where Rose was showering.

He looked over on the bed to find a book she had been reading. He crept up to the shower and flung the door open.

The vision was blurred and flicking like a broken TV set. He pulled her from the shower, he could vaguely hear screams from her but he kept passing in and out of consciousness. He slammed her into the wardrobes and smashed glass around her, screaming at her as she lay there on the floor naked and sobbing with fear

"How did you get out?" she screamed into his face.

"Fuck you Rose I Didn't want to wake up I told you to leave me alone…I fucking feel something I have tried so hard to lock away and you have to do this to me now!"

"What are you talking about?"

"I have …I have my father's illness Jekyll and Hyde you remember my unpredictability?"

He grabbed her hair and flung her on to the bed

"No no please Sebastian"

He threw the covers off the bed and threw the draws out of the cabinet before running to the living room and smashing the vase of roses from the mantel piece. Screaming in a roar of rage he grabbed Rose off the bed and dragged her by her hair to the kitchen

"You feel how I feel Rose?" His face searing red and spitting as he roared in her face.

"I do Sebastian, I do but I haven't hurt you I'm not who you think I am"

Sebastian grabbed a knife and held her wrists down she screaming, he muffled her with his hand and cut deep into her wrists, as her blood poured from her wrists he kissed her blood then kissed Rose on her lips…

"Taste the disdain of yourself?"

As he kissed, her Rose was mumbling something

"Wait wait wait please Sebastian I'm I'm…"

He sat on her chest so she could not move from him. He held her wrists and covered her mouth again he could see she was losing consciousness. Blood was pouring fast from her as he cut length ways down her wrist…the door banged and he heard Ralf shouting to open up Rose faded out and the door was forced open by the police they ran in and pulled Sebastian off Rose.

Sebastian stood there with his head in his hands. "She's fucking pregnant I've tried to kill her and I'm fucking delusional."

He closed both their files and took a seat, breathing uncontrollably a sense of panic struck him. He quickly got up from the chair and made copies of the files, he also searched for both of their parents files.

He opened his own and read that his father had killed his mother. Sebastian fell back on his chair, he had thought that his mother had killed herself, he put his head in his hands and sobbed hard.

His chest hurting, he was inconsolable. Shaking his head in rage he slammed the folder shut and carried on copying quickly, tears streaming he wiped them away. Furious his thoughts reran the past in his head, his father dragging her body around the room.

He puts the files back in the rightful places shuts the cabinets and locked them.

He then sat down again, put his head on the desk his temples pulsating attempting to process all that he had found out. He felt loose paper under his palm of his hands, he looked up and found a pen. He began to write.

DAMAGED:

A long time ago in what feels like another age. Your raw energy has left my body pulsing like waves flowing away in ripples from the great energy that is you.

Waiting once more for a gap in your flawless wall of protection to once again sweep in and make myself yours.

I long for your playful smile, lost to the valley of doubts and circumstances.

I know but one thing with all my heart that I love you.

Scribbling the note quickly he folded it and put it in his pocket.

He looked at his watch it had only shifted by a minute since he has entered the office.

"That's not possible."

Tapping his watch he looked at the door and it was still dark out. He sighed and walked from the room locking it behind him.

Looking round to see where he was he ran past his room to put the keys back on the reception and ran back to his room. As he got closer he began walking holding his chest to keep the files in place.

"Sorry I went to the toilet my stomach isn't too good."

"Oh dear Mr Lawrence well eat your food and I'll have the doctors look at you later today."

"Thank you so much."

The nurse shut the door and Sebastian fell to his bed his head spinning trying to keep himself together…he desperately wanted to see Rose.

He took the files from his chest and flicked through Rose's again.

"I have done this to her? I am a monster and she's pregnant with my child!" He whispered to himself.

He felt his body wilt and energy sapped from him. He looked out the window but his mind was elsewhere. His eyes tired he climbed to his bed sat on his note pad and puts pen to paper.

MY LIFE IS YOURS:

My life is yours. No…that doesn't even begin to get to the core of what you mean to me. If you were pulled from me it would be far more then feeling like I've lost half of myself…I am little more than a familiar to you. You are the reason and purpose of who I am, my life and all that resides within it. sit here wanting to hold your hand and wanting to feel your pulse echoing through me, you are a Titan.

Your energy pulsing and flowing within me like music.

Nothing so limited like the waves of the ocean, boundless to the eye and awe-inspiring.

I am but a candle next to the sea of flame that is your energy…I can feel you in my heart burning, aside from my discomfort my pain. You pulling it into you, use it to fuel your flame that keeps me warm and safe. I am bound to you with chains and rope, with heart and mind, with soul and spirit.

God could demand I leave you and I could stand against even them to stay by your side. When I have you…I am unstoppable, without you…I am like a man grown suddenly rich finally used to luxury and then to have it torn from me.

 I look at things I once enjoyed with distaste and boredom nothing can compare to you nothing could hold you down when you spread your wings you are an angel my angel and I will never let you go....

Sebastian's eyes were closing and he dropped his pen to the floor and passed out asleep.

THE WORLDS END.

The light was dull when the nurses pulled his curtains back. He got up rubbing his eyes, his diary and pens fell to the floor

"Shit sorry"

"It's okay Mr Lawrence I'll pick them up"

Giving a shy look, he had a plan cemented in his mind.

The nurse walked from his room, he got up and changed quick and peeked out of his door. He glanced at his watch to see if it was midday.

He had the files tucked under his top with some of his diary entries. Hoping that no one was guarding her room. Peeking round the corner of her room he heard the doctors come out he looked at it more and saw her room was clear. He rushed in and shut the door behind him but he stopped at the vision of her. He had not seen her for over a month and her skin as delicate as a petal she laid there peacefully, her hair dark as chocolate. He rushed over to her bed and put the case files and diary entries under her mattress.

He looked over her face and smelt her familiar skin. He sat on the chair and held her hand feeling the rough skin of where he had cut her he ran his fingers over then he looked to her and put his face next to hers whispering,

"Jesus Rose I'm so sorry if you can hear me I'm so sorry for what I'm about to do.

I love you with all my heart and I am recovering I don't mean for you to lose me, his face against hers he felt a sudden rush of sadness.

"I actually feel love"

A rush hit again and he burst into tears he sobbed hard deep into her chest holding her close to him he shook her body.

"You told me the truth, even when it hurt, you knew a lie was worse, that's love.

When I was at my worst you would still be by my side, that's love You taught me to help others and by doing so I also found happiness. That's love. He stroked her hair and kissed her lips, he was palpable with love. He wept into her neck, whispering into her ear, hoping her eyes would flicker with the word he repeated to her. He kissed her chest and hands and every fingertip.

"Please dear god don't let this end I want this to be everything" Sebastian's thoughts came at him with a rush.

"We are all gods we decide our fate…"

A nurse knocked on Rose's door Sebastian held Rose closer to him knowing what was going to happen next…

"Sorry we need to enter Rose's room and wash her down I'll enter."

As the nurse did, she gasped to see Sebastian curled round Rose sobbing she dropped the hot water bowel and shouted for security.

"Please security get him quick, Mr Lawrence step away from Miss Banks."

"No I can't, I haven't hurt her, or the baby please just let me stay with her please"

The security rushed in and Sebastian shouted screaming and kicking away from her body. Suddenly Rose went into cardiac arrest and more nurses came rushing into the room.

Sebastian had a flash back of when Rose's mother died.

"No Rose please this wasn't me saying goodbye, I want you back, I need you back."

His cries echoed the hospital halls.

PAST COMETH.

"You can't do this I love her please don't do this to me I can't handle my life without her please don't do this to me."

The security's guards pushed and pulled him away from Rose and into the door handcuffing him. They marched him to his room kicking, screaming and finally un cuffed him. His door was locked behind them. Sebastian flew at the window hitting it hard and screaming he threw his fists into the wall trying to break free, he stood there out of breath, exhausted and turned to a mirror on the wall half hanging off. Trying to calm his senses he wiped his tears away abruptly his face changed distorted to his father's figure.

It was now in front of him and his anger shot out. He punched the mirror, he fell against the wall and slid down it, he grasped a piece of glass in one hand, he put his head against the wall closed his eyes… Visions would hit at him like as heavy as stone.

Where his mother would sooth him to sleep stroking his hair and his feelings of peace warmed his soul.

His memory flashed back to where his dad would hit him and impales his arms with a fire poker and beat his face with it.

Sebastian would scream to him.

"Why haven't you just killed me yet?"

It would flash back to his mother washing his wounds, as she wept, her tears fell to his skin making him seethe as it hurt from the salt.

She smiled through the stream that escaped her eyes, he would look up to her and promise her it would all be over soon and she would look down to him and whisper

"We are the destiny for all our fates and it lies in our hands only son, this I have no control over, I run, he finds me but I love your father above all else"

Sebastian sat there with a confused look on his face

"You'll understand one day Sebastian trust me."

Sebastian opened his eyes and took the glass he drew the piece hard into his skin. Feeling every inch of it drag across his veins, he clenched his jaw to try not to make a sound.

Watching his blood pour he wrote on the walls "FEEL", he did the other wrist he stood there feeling pain like never before. He slid down the wall.

He could see reality fading in and out, the face of his mother would fade and reappear, his mind at peace for once.

Peace fell over him and a vision of Rose was at the forefront of his mind her hair blowing in the wind as she ran with their child in the woods playing hide and seek and Sebastian would be watching from afar sniffing the faint scent of Rose. He smiled with a happy feeling...

He took the piece of mirror one last time and held it to his throat, he cut deep and across it he fell to the side and watched as reality and life slipped by, death was standing behind him and said

"Take my hand and follow me, your hour of much needed rest from this world has come."

A faint sound of feet running towards his room and alarms been sounded around the hospital as his door slammed open and the doctors lifted him up and onto a bed. He was being carried to the operating theatre.

As Sebastian's life drained away, Rose grew stronger and her baby's distress signs were getting better. Sebastian was bleeding out fast and they could not stop the gushing. As he took his final breath. Rose's eyes flickered open choking on the apparatus that was in her mouth the nurses rushed over and helped her.

"Doctors please hurry Rose is awake!"

Sebastian lay there on the surgery table the surgeons stood back as the doctor called time of death looking at the clock it was ten in the evening.

Rose was laying down looking around the room she was disoriented and tried to grasp her bearings. Feeling her stomach the baby was making progress and started kicking her, her head in a spin.

"Where is Sebastian? He is my partner. Do you know where he is?"

The nurses looked at each other.

"I'm sorry Miss Banks Mr Lawrence died a few hours ago.

"No, no not my Sebastian, he is six feet tall dark with black hair he wears gold rimmed glasses!" she said sternly

"Miss Banks he passed away.

She sat there in a trance, trying to make sense of the information.

Rose began crying and felt her wrists…her chest was wet

"Why is my chest wet?" she says sobbing.

"Miss Banks…there is a lot to tell you"

"Where is Sebastian?"

"Miss Banks…"

"WHERE IS SEBASTIAN?"

"He passed away …he was curled over your body as you were in a coma crying on your chest."

"No no no you lie he can't be dead...he cried for the first time for me!" She shook her head in disbelief.

"We're so sorry..."

"Where is he how did he die?"

"Please Miss Ba..."

Before the nurse could say another word Rose got up from her bed falling back to the floor the nurse tried to help her up she battered them off.

"I'm fine take me to him now please I beg"

"But he tried to..." cutting them off from talking any further, she interrupted

"What kill me? I'm fully aware, take me to him"

They helped her into her robe and down the corridor; she stood outside the door of where he lay on the operating table.

"Can I say my goodbyes to him?" she asks in a sullen tone to nurses by her side.

The nurses nodded and walked away, Rose stood there looking on at his body. Through the door the surgeons still stood around him, she walked in slowly the creak of the door echoed around the room and a smell of disinfectant hits her nostrils hard.

"Sorry you can't be in here alone" the surgeon turned to her, as he is sewing up his throat.

"He's my partner please can I say my goodbye" she says quietly

"We can't leave you alone in the room with him so we will just stand in the back" they said in unison. The surgeons looked to one another, and all nodded in agreement to leave her be for a while. They slowly walked to the back of the room.

YOUR HAND.

The room was silent as night, standing there her baby kicking her she walked towards Sebastian. He lay there in his blood that still dripped heavily from his body. She shakes her head, tears free fall from her onto his body.

"What have you done my love?" she asks looking at his body intensely.

She took his blood soaked hand, and kisses it; gently rubbing it against her face.

"I don't care what you did to me... I loved you, and what I saw wasn't you. I know this...and you couldn't have waited for me?!"

She sobbed and fell to his chest she whispered in his ear.

"You finally felt love and I'm so proud of you. I would go with you but I have our child...it is a girl... I'm naming her Faith she's well again and due to be born soon."

She closed her eyes tight and tears fell from the heavens.

"I can't leave you, you know nothing, you didn't know I was pregnant and I'm sure if you did you wouldn't have killed yourself!"

The surgeons walked over quietly and slowly. Rose looked over her shoulder then back to Sebastian.

"I will love you forever and one day we will meet again and I will wait for you"

The surgeon walked over and put one hand on her shoulder to console her.

"I'm sorry I'd have to ask you to leave now we need to get him to the mortuary"

Rose closed her eyes for a little longer as they took the body from the room she opened them up to find he was gone. The nurses came back in to escort her back to her room she fell to her bed tired and distraught from what had happened. As she shifted her torso she felt a scratch. Looking under her leg there was a file sticking out, she pulled it from underneath and saw the words

"Case files and diaries."

She stopped crying and wiped her tears, a nurse entered the room and she quickly hid them behind her back.

"Sorry nurse can I have some privacy please I just want to be alone for now"

The nurse nodded

"Of course I'm sorry I just wanted to say that the doctors will be in to asses you soon."

"Thank you but can you hold them off for today please."

"Of course no problem," the nurse said and quietly closed the door.

Vicious circle

Rose took the files from behind her and settled into her bed, she flicked open Sebastian's file it read;

Sebastian had been married to a woman named Jane Bross, who is now flight attendant. Due to his problem he had tried to harm Jen and since the violent tendencies did not wain, it caused a breakdown in their marriage.

Rose shook her head, everything fell into place. The flight she was on and why she had said she had never seen her and Sebastian so happy, the phone call she made to Jen when she was worried about Sebastian's outbursts, the abrupt end to the call, she read on.

He had no emotions feeling or remorse those of traits of a psychopath but was diagnosed with hypnosis acting as psychosis. He was treated with therapy but to no avail, it never helped and he escaped the hospital.

She put his file down on the floor and two others fell out

It read Mrs **** Lawrence, Mr ***** Lawrence

His mother was a PHD psychologist in human behaviour retired; his father was a raging alcoholic with no further details other then the rehabs he had been in and out of.

His father had killed his mother. Rose put her hand over her mouth in disgust. She looked upon the files spread over her bed and shook her head trying to stifle her crying whimpers, she shook head and closed her eyes tears streaming she knew it was possibly this fact that he had killed himself.

She began slowly opening her file to read that her mother Mrs Hope Banks was a spiritualist with schizophrenia, her father Mr **** Banks was a scientist who also suffered from depression and suicidal tendencies.

Her father committed a successful suicide causing her mother's schizophrenia to go into full pelt, with hallucinations and voices that would make her hit rose on a regular basis thinking it was someone else.

Her past hit her like a rock. Looking to the back pieces of paper fell out of the back scattered all over the floor was love poems Sebastian's feelings and emotions.

she sprawled out to the floor to pick them up and ended up sitting there reading every last one with tears streaming from her. Sobbing her heart out she buried her head into her hands.

Ten years later.

Rose had given birth to a beautiful baby girl naming her Faith Eva banks. She had moved out of Sebastian's apartment and had released Ralf of his duties, she moved to the countryside to escape the brawl and chaos of the city.

Faith was ten years old; Rose never spoke to Faith much about her father or anything that had happened to them over the course of the years. Faith was too young to understand and so Rose was leaving it all to when she was old enough to accept things.

Rose had only briefly told Faith she had a father named Sebastian who had passed away of natural causes, which Faith understood and accepted.

One evening night fell and Rose had taken her out of the bath and dried her, she popped her into her pyjamas and kissed her goodnight.

"Sweet dreams beautiful I love you."

As she walked away from the bedroom, she could feel her heart pounding fast, the room span and she gripped the doorframe to keep her balance, feeling faint she sat on the floor.

"Mum!" Faith shouted she got out of her bed urgently and faced Rose.

"Mum look at me, stare at me and concentrate on my voice okay?!"

Rose nodded still trying to catch her breath, and gripping onto her chest as it tightened.

"Mum can you hear me?"

Rose nodded back.

"Some fun facts about space and planets okay?" Faiths smiled enthusiastically. "Venus spins in the opposite direction to most planets," she paused trying to think quick to try distract her mums anxious mind.

Rose's face changed from panicked to distraught; in her quick breathing, she managed to talk.

"What.....are......you.....doing?"

Faith looked confused.

"I was told to distract your mind when you was having an anxiety attack, so please focus on me" Faith was getting frustrated as she could not see Rose improving only worsening but she perservered.

"Neptune orbits the sun once every…"

Rose tried to get up abruptly, and interrupts Faith talking. With concern on her face and still mid anxiety attack she asked.

"No this can't be, who is this? Who told you this? I've never…..told you anything of this?"

Faith was impatient watching her mum getting no better, with panic in her voice.

"Mum for god sake! Please just sit down you're going to make yourself worse what is wrong with you?"

Rose managed to stand on her feet staring close into Faiths face she quietly asks.

"Where, who, when, I, don't under…."

Faith caught her as Rose passed out on her.

Rose woke up looking to the ceiling of the living room with the fan whistling around above her, Faiths face appeared above hers.

"Hey you! Glad you're back."

Rose closed her eyes again for a moment and reopened them slowly.

"Faith, who told you to calm me the way you did?"

SEBASTIAN IN MIND.

Faith looked at her with a blank expression and turned away from her.

"Please Faith, it scares me how you know because there are only two people who know of those things and I've never told you, so please tell me who told you?

Faith turned back to look at Rose and replied, "why does it matter how I know mum?"

She took her hand and looked her in the eyes.

"Because my beautiful girl the only two people who know of this are dead."

Faith bowed her head and tears fell heavily onto her hands. Rose raised her chin up to look her in the eyes.

"Please Faith tell me, I won't judge you, I'm just curious."

Faith hesitated at first.

"I….I have dreams mum, I've had them since I was six years old, dad would be there in them It was of you and dad; I was standing by the entrance of a door and I saw you in a red dress that had a long flowing trail. Daddy was on the other side of the room he was dressed in a blue velvet jacket, I saw him walk over to you from across the room and you passed out, then I left you both."

Rose shunted back on the sofa rubbing her eyes and face to wake up from what felt like a dream.

"No Faith you couldn't possibly know that!"

"Was it a bad dream I had mum?"

"Faith I have never told you of how me and your father met for the second time, it's only something me and your father knew."

"I have dreams of this, I have for some time now."

Rose was stunned; she just stared at Faith for what felt like a lifetime. She touched her face and smiled.

Faith continued

"You were in a red gown your trail is so long and flowing that it looks magnificent and you was standing looking out of a window on a winters day. Snow fell in slowly and a man who looks like my father is walking towards, you he kisses your shoulder and he whispers in your ear…" Faiths voice trailed off.

Rose looked at Faith with intensity and curiosity.

"What's up Faith, what does your father whisper to me?"

Her heart now pounding into her ears to hear a secret only one person knows.

Faith had tears in her eyes and began to sob.

"He says…he says, FEEL!"

She fell to her knees in front of Faith, and grabbed her face gently and staring into her eyes as if looking for something, whispering gently into her daughter's face...

"Sebastian?"

Faiths eyes blinked and her pupils dilated. She nodded. Rose closed her eyes and took her daughters hand, put it to her face and kissed her palm as tears streamed from her eyes.

"Sebastian, you really meant what you said? You would really be with me for eternity..."

Faith sits closer to Rose's ear

"I will love you for eternity and I will take many forms but dreams are all I have for now, until we meet again."

Faith sat on the floor and raised her mother's face to hers.

"I finally feel, face the past before the past faces you."

Rose looked confused and she turned away from Faith she could not think what he meant. Rose looked to Faith again and as she did, something sharp hit her head, Rose passed out.

With a knock on the door Faith opened the door to be faced with Ralf, Jen and James.

Printed in Great Britain
by Amazon